MW01005547

STARBORN

A mystical tale

JOHN NELSON

REVISED EDITION

THE
DONNING COMPANY
PUBLISHERS
NORFOLK/VIRGINIA BEACH

STARBORN

A mystical tale

JOHN NELSON

Copyright © 1978, 1986 by John Nelson

All rights reserved, including the right to reproduce this
book in any form whatsoever without permission in
writing from the publisher, except for brief passages in
connection with a review. For information, write:
   The Donning Company/Publishers
   5659 Virginia Beach Boulevard
   Norfolk, Virginia 23502

Library of Congress Cataloging-in-Publication Data

Nelson, John
   Starborn.
   (A Unilaw library book)
   I. Title.
   PZ4.N42715St   [PS3564.E465]   813:5:4
   ISBN 0-915442-68-X   78-22108

First Printing—November 1978
Second Printing—May 1982
Third Printing—December 1984
Revised Edition—October 1986

Printed in the United States of America

PART ONE

ONE

While lying in his crib, Edward looked up through the nursery window at the Sun shining overhead, and wished he were there once again. There were so many disadvantages to being mortal. At the mercy of the weather, he was subject to the heat and cold, burning up in the summer and freezing in the winter. He also had to eat to sustain himself, express his thoughts in words instead of direct transference. His feeble body would grow old and eventually fall apart. Fortunately, as a newborn infant, Edward was able to spend most of his time sleeping and dreaming of worlds more compatible than this wretched place.

Edward's first mistake was returning to a world he had left long ago. And he was having such a great time zipping around the Milky Way, visiting friends here and there, racing comets, throwing shooting stars. Edward had left behind much unfinished business, but after so many bad experiences, he had decided to take a vacation for several centuries and hopefully gain a new perspective on his old problems. Edward did have a lot to reexamine.

That was when Rana and Cara decided to incarnate along with some of their other soul mates. They were excited about many startling new terrestrial developments, saying it would be one of the most important periods in earth history. Edward didn't agree. All he could see were resurrected Atlanteans running about with their fission bombs and laser weapons, preparing to destroy the world again.

Edward didn't want any part of it, but after they had reincarnated, it became quite lonely for him up there zipping around all by himself. He had other friends to visit, plenty of things to occupy his time, but still his existence was incomplete. They had always been together even in their fifty lifetimes on Earth. Edward missed them both more than he wanted to admit.

Finally, and at the last minute, Edward decided to join them. They were going to need him down there. Everybody was sure to take their brief sojourn far too seriously. No doubt they would need a little of his cosmic humor to liven up the situation. Edward now had to make some fast arrangements for his return, or find himself ten or fifteen years behind them. In the past it was important to incarnate in the same general vicinity if you planned to retain contact with old friends. But with modern air travel that wouldn't be a problem. Now oceans couldn't separate you if the bond was strong enough.

Edward found himself in an unique position. He had the

whole world from which to choose his parents. Preferably his choice would be based on old karmic ties that needed further work, but that wasn't his prime consideration. This time he wanted parents who were well-off. He had already gone through his poor cycle, and that wasn't much fun. And he preferred being smart and good-looking, so they would need the right genetic makeup.

Edward spent a considerable amount of time scanning pregnant mothers worldwide, but couldn't uncover any great prospects. Time was slipping by rapidly, and he had to make a choice or fall hopelessly behind the others. When Mary got pregnant, Edward decided to go in through her. He had hoped to do better, but at least they had always gotten along fairly well, and he did have a few things to work out with her husband, Adam. And besides he liked the vibration of their last name: Doolittle.

This was where he made his second mistake. For while preparing for reentry, Edward forgot to disconnect his soul memory. When they pulled him out into the cold cruel world and slapped his behind, he could very easily have turned around and told the doctor to keep his hands to himself.

TWO

There he was, hanging upside down and screaming his lungs out. It was not a very auspicious beginning, but certainly appropriate. For Edward was an artist, poet, philosopher and sometime cosmic clown, who had suddenly found himself in the body of a newborn baby. Birth into the physical plane was always the most agonizing cosmic experience; it was as if you had compressed the Sun into the head of a pin. Eventually you recovered as vague memories of what you were rapidly gave way to what you were becoming: an earthbound ego.

With his memory still intact, Edward had access to the knowledge of all the lives he had lived. At various times and in various places, he had been the poet laureate of ancient Xeba, a student of Socrates, an apprentice to Leonardo da Vinci, and a con man in 19th century Paris. He had spun these and many more lives in the course of time, and now the memory of all his past efforts, his deep karmic connections with family and friends, would plague him through this life.

When Edward realized what had happened to him, he gave such a fit that the nurses finally had to tie him down in a miniature straightjacket. It was going to be hard enough living with his past mistakes, but also knowing his true nature as an infinite being was going to be almost unbearable. How could he possibly identify with making money, chasing women, watching football games, playing the stock market?

He wasn't Edward Doolittle, the son of Adam and Mary Doolittle. He was a star child, as expansive as the universe and as old as time itself. How was he going to play games with the children in the neighborhood, when he was used to playing dodge ball with meteors? How was he going to sit and listen to a lecture on a particular period of history, when he had participated in the events described?

Edward was never one for details, but this was absurd. His first problem was how to survive the next couple of years as a baby. He would quickly have to learn how to act and needed a whole repertoire of baby sounds to use instead of cursing every time he was stuck with a pin. Edward went back in his memory to his past incarnations as a woman and a mother, and he picked up a few pointers, but when he tried to remember himself as a baby, the memories were far too subjective for him to gather any useful information.

At the hospital he tried to check out the other babies, but he never had a very good vantage point lying on his back most of the time. He would have to wait until his parents took him home, and there he would do the necessary research behind his mother's back. So, how was he going to pass the time, lie there and stare at the ceiling?

One of the more trying aspects of life in a nursery was this never-ending babble of baby sounds. Edward could speak over thirty ancient and modern languages, but unfortunately this was not one of them. Just thinking the sounds intelligible made Edward wonder if his dilemma might not be due to a cosmic mishap which affected other babies as well. Maybe he had some allies out there in nurseryland?

Late one night, after the nurse had made her rounds, Edward called out to the others, "Is anybody out there in the same fix?" The infants were all fast asleep, and nobody stirred. So, at the top of his psychically projected voice, Edward yelled, "Okay kiddies, talk to me!" He was answered by a chorus of cries, and before the nurse returned, he repeated this question, but it was to no avail. His situation was apparently unique; it appeared that Fate had played one of its better jokes on him.

When Edward finally realized the utter hopelessness of his predicament, he became very angry. What had he done to deserve such a fate? So he played around, didn't take existence seriously, and had fallen far behind in his spiritual development. But, nevertheless, he was a sweet soul and had never been mean or cruel to anyone. What would be gained by losing himself in the circus of life? Several nights later, while Edward was brooding in his crib, he received an unexpected visitor.

"Edward Doolittle," the voice quietly called out.

"Yeah, who's there?"

A ghostly vision now appeared beside Edward's crib, and he covered his eyes with tiny pink hands. Finally, he peeked out to discover his old Soul Guide, Tolan.

"Wow, don't scare me like that. I thought you were one of those spooky nurses."

"I was listening to your thoughts, and felt it might help if I clarified a few points," Tolan said with a disapproving scowl.

"School time," he replied.

"Yes, Edward. And for you it's still kindergarten." When this remark had the desired effect, Tolan continued. "Now, fate has nothing to do with your present predicament, nor did the Higher Forces pull any of those proverbial strings to place you in it."

"Well, I sure in the hell didn't do it."

"On the contrary. If you review your reentry, you'll discover that in your rush to come into the Doolittle family, for your own selfish reasons, you forgot to cut off your soul memory."

"Aren't there natural checks to prevent that from happening?"

"Yes, for less evolved souls. But it's an option open to you. Some vary the degree of residual memory, but in your case, you ran the limits. And now you have to make the most of it."

"Yeah, well, what if I accidentally catch pneumonia and pass on?"

"There are no accidents, Edward. And you know how suicide is treated under natural law. You'd just have to come back and go through it again."

Edward started to chew on his nonexistent fingernails.

"That's just great. So, what am I supposed to do for the next seventy years, walk around down here with the rest of these clowns and pretend it's for real?"

"If you learn to love, yourself and others, all else will fall in place."

"That's certainly original," Edward said with heavy sarcasm.

"I must go for now, Edward. But, when you need further counseling, I will return. Peace be with you, my son."

After Tolan's visit, realizing he was stuck down here, Edward's already cranky disposition turned sour. He would try to adapt himself to this rather distressing situation, but that didn't mean he couldn't have any fun with it. His first target was a nurse who would cheerfully wake him up every morning with, "And how you today, little Eddie?" After a while, it got tiring. One morning, when they were alone, Edward replied, "Pretty good, and how are you, big nurse?" Startled, she jumped back from the crib as Edward added, "Gugu poop-poo on you, lady."

This incident caused quite a stir in the nursery, as Nurse Barton brought in one doctor after another to examine her talking wonder. Edward would silently lie there in all his sweet innocence, babbling away in baby talk. Finally, she was given an extended vacation after they found her in a linen closet talking to herself. The other nurses were now leery of Edward, and this was fine with him. Occasionally a nurse would sneeze in the nursery, and he would reply with a "God bless you." The nurse would start to offer her thanks until she realized she was alone with only the infants present.

Edward became quite notorious in a very short time,

and the nurses were increasingly reluctant to tend to him. One day, when they neglected to feed him on time, Edward let out with, "Me want food, fast." But eventually this game got old, and outside of whistling at a nurse who bent over too far, Edward behaved himself. For the time being, he tried to sleep as much as possible. It was only in dreaming that he could slip out of his earthbound body and once again experience, if only for a short time, the infinity of his total being.

THREE

To be free, to shed your physical body and soar out of the Earth plane, pass the Moon, and then picking up speed, faster and faster, through the Sun to the stars, leaving galaxy after galaxy behind you, plunging deeper and deeper into the absolute infinity of the universe; to expand past its boundless limits with each beat of creation, to contract into nothingness in one moment and be born again as the universe in the next; to be one with the eternal flow of all life, to want not and have all, to think not and know all, to feel nothing and experience everything. . . .

And the nurses wondered why Edward slept so much. If they knew of his illicit journeys, no doubt they would've kept him up all night. However, after several trips, that was soon unnecessary because the agonizing pain of coming back into his body was too much of a shock. He slept, but for now it would be the sleep of sweet nothingness. To be constantly reminded of what he was would only limit his ability to contend with whom he was becoming.

Edward was a boundless infinite being, who was now trapped in a limited mortal body. He could no longer merely think of a place and instantly be there; he now had to fly a plane or drive a car. If he was interested in a particular period of earth history, he could no longer slip back in time and live it as it was happening; he now had to read about it in a history book. If he saw an unusual creature he wanted to study, or a distant object that excited his curiosity, he could no longer become it and fully experience its being; he now had to study it under a microscope or view it through a telescope.

If you didn't know of life elsewhere, you might get excited by this world's possibilities. Edward knew a freedom only imagined down here, and now this shackled existence would be unbearable. There would be some consolation if it were merely a memory, but Edward still had many of his psychic powers intact. He could still experience enough of that other world to know that this one was definitely not for him. Edward slept, but it was a restless sleep.

While he slept, a new earthbound problem was gathering force. Her name was Dr. Abigail Peterson, and she would soon threaten Edward's right to life, liberty and the pursuit of nothingness. Dr. Peterson was the chairperson of the National Council on Child Resources, and she was determined to make the children of America and eventually the world: bigger, better and brighter. She fervidly believed that this generation of children could make the world safe for happiness. But first they must be made aware of this grave responsibility.

To indoctrinate them and eventually to lead her army, Abigail would need a strong leader, a master among children. She knew he had come in at this time to fulfill her destiny and she would find him and rally him to the cause. Dr. Peterson had a theory on genetic mutation which stated that once in every hundred million births a mutant was born. This genius was intellectually far superior to his contemporaries and talented beyond belief. But far too often, before he could develop his abilities and assert his superiority, he was crushed by a system threatened by his mere existence.

Abigail would rescue her little genius from such a plight, discipline his mind, hone his talents and develop his body. Together they would save the world. Inspired by such a noble ambition, she was completely out of her mind, but like many full-fledged maniacs she was able to level all opposition with her shrill insistence. Across the country she had a network of pediatricians taking blood samples, measuring craniums, watching and waiting for nature to slip and deliver them a Messiah.

When Dr. Gabe Addison heard about all the strange happenings in the third floor nursery, he decided to detain the mother and her child while he conducted an investigation with Abigail in mind. He put Edward under constant observation, took depositions from all the nurses involved, and finally rigged the nursery with sensitive microphones and long-range cameras. Edward sensed the intrusive nature of this hidden activity, and for once he behaved himself. However, Dr. Addison eventually caught him off guard, taping a garbled recording of Edward talking in his sleep. Excited by this monumental discovery, he immediately called in Dr. Peterson.

Sitting in Dr. Addison's office, Abigail played the recording several times while trying to hide her growing excitement. Finally, she looked up at her colleague and cautiously asked, "Well, Gabe, what do you make of it?"

"I'm not sure, Abigail. A baby's vocal cords are fairly developed at twelve months, and I've heard a child at eighteen months with incredible diction. But it was still baby talk, not a dialogue about the weather conditions on Jupiter." Gabe took a puff on his pipe, "Physiologically, it's impossible, not to mention the implied . . . mental development."

"But we heard the child speaking."

"I know, but I can't explain it," Gabe said in exasperation. "Language is developed from long tedious experience. The child associates objects with sounds and forms a meaningful connection. What experience can a three-week-old infant have?"

"But what if he is able to tap the racial memory of our species? If Carl Jung is right, all man's knowledge, his accumulated experience down through the ages, is locked up in our subconscious mind."

"That would be simply incredible," Gabe said, taken aback by this startling idea. "Do you know what that would mean to science?"

"To hell with science. What would it mean to the human race if we could duplicate this mutation process? Hopefully, a new species of man more advanced and peace-loving than the present variety."

"In other words, you want me to keep our little discovery a secret."

"For the time being, let's give the child a chance to develop on his own without being put into some kind of scientific zoo."

Abigail had other plans for Edward that could do without Dr. Addison's interference. He had done an admirable job finding her child and would be well rewarded, but Gabe did not understand her vision of a new race of human beings, and his collaboration would only slow her down. However, Abigail's first problem was convincing Edward to cooperate with her.

Several days later, while Dr. Addison was busy elsewhere, Abigail had an unsuspecting nurse wheel Edward's crib into a private examination room. When they were left alone, she picked the infant up and placed him on her knee.

"Okay, Edward. I know you can understand me, so don't give me any of that gugu crap. Let me put it this way. You either play along with me, or I'm going to make life pretty damn impossible for you. Now listen carefully. For the next ten years, you're going to be at the mercy of a lot of stupid people, and if they haven't crushed you by then and you decide to go out on your own, the world will eat you alive. There is no place for you, Edward. You're a freak, a mutant, a threat to them.

"But, if you work with me, I can have you in the body of a twenty-year-old man by the age of eight. With hormone and vitamin treatments, you can be free of this clumsy infantile body and enjoy physical relationships while others your age are still reading dirty magazines.

"And what about your mind, Edward? Are you going to be stimulated by a grade school curriculum? Next week we can start studying higher mathematics, and by the age of ten you will have the equivalent of a Ph.D. in physics. And your feelings, Edward. What about them? You'll be disgusted with the people around you and their meager abilities, and you'll grow cold and heartless. A misanthrope by the age of twelve.

"And just think about the power. You could rule the world by the age of fifteen. The next Alexander. If the world is to prevent a nuclear Armageddon, it must be united by a strong, wise leader. You are that man, Edward. Are you going to claim your rightful destiny, or dwindle away into nothingness? Yours is the choice. Tell me what it will be?"

Edward thought that just when life looked unbearable, this maniac shows up to confirm his worst suspicions. A raving mad Joan of Arc was exactly what he needed right now. And yet her scheme sounded only too familiar. How many times down through history had he heard such wild-eyed machinations? The world hadn't changed very much after all; maniacs were still trying to legislate morality or feed it to a subjugated humanity. If these reformers were really interested in the welfare of humanity, they would help raise the consciousness of the people, make them aware of their true nature as spiritual beings, instead of raising their banner over the next generation of well-fed slaves. Edward wanted no part of this crazy scheme; power had never enticed him in the past, and was even less appealing in this present guise. He answered Dr. Peterson with a juicy stream of baby babble.

"I take this as your answer, Edward. And I must say I'm a little disappointed in you. But our crusade is more important than the selfish desires of one small person, and so I cannot allow you to desert the cause. Just remember, Edward. I'm going to be there watching and waiting, and as soon as you make a slip, I'm going to reveal you and let the world bring you back to us."

FOUR

It was soon time to take Edward home from the hospital. He looked forward to leaving. Although he had taken measures to prevent another nocturnal slip of the tongue, Dr. Peterson continued to sneak into the nursery at all hours of the night trying to catch him talking in his sleep again. When Abigail's efforts were frustrated, she decided to take another approach. She called Mrs. Doolittle in for a consultation the day of her release from the hospital.

"Now, Mary. I don't want to frighten you, but we have every reason to believe that little Edward is extremely precocious."

"I can believe it. Why, the first time I held him, he looked up at me as if he knew me, knew where he was at. It was really spooky. Now, is that possible?" Mary asked.

"Not hardly, but we do expect him to develop very

rapidly, if not that fast," Abigail said, trying to play down Mary's astute observation. "What I would like you to do, is watch him very carefully and as soon as anything . . . unusual occurs, write it down and date it."

"So you think he'll walk and talk ahead of time?"

"I can assure you of that," Abigail said with a little too much confidence, and Mary looked at her curiously. "I mean, we would expect that, but other things might take you by surprise. Don't get excited. Just remember that every child has an unlimited potential, but some can express more of it than others."

"Exactly what should I look for?" Mary asked nervously.

"Drawing at an early age, teaching himself to play the piano. Edward is definitely prodigy material. Are there any artists in your family?"

"My husband's an architect, and that speaks for itself."

"Good. The seed is planted in fertile ground, as they say. Anyway, go through his wastepaper basket every day, leave writing paper and crayons out, record any sessions on the piano. Things like that."

"I've always had talents that were left unfulfilled. Maybe my little boy will express them for me."

Abigail handed Mrs. Doolittle her card as she got up to leave. "Here's my number, Mary. Please call me as soon as anything unusual develops. Otherwise, I'll pay you a visit once a year hereafter." Dr. Peterson planned to use the Doolittles to build up a case history against their son, one she could use to coerce Edward into working with her.

Later that afternoon, as Mary was leaving the hospital, Abigail stopped her at the front door to give Edward a kiss goodbye. When nobody was watching, he gave her a big wink in return.

After several days, when Edward was comfortably situated at home, he decided not to waste any more time and do his research on babies. His mother kept a few baby books on the nightstand in her bedroom. One afternoon he threw a fit when she tried to put him back in his crib, and he wouldn't let up until she laid him down on the bed. When Mary fell asleep lying beside him, Edward crawled over to the nightstand and pulled the top book off the stack.

He began to read about the very complex world of babyland where he was temporarily stranded. Edward was an actor playing a role, and now he would carefully have to read the script to know when to walk and when to talk. It was more complicated than he had ever imagined, and he became deeply absorbed in his book.

Edward heard a noise and turned to find his mother sitting on the edge of the bed watching him. He smiled at her, and with a shrug of his shoulders, Edward turned back to his book. Mary watched as his eyes ran across the page, his lips forming the words as he read, and then heard a faintly spoken word. She tried to scream, but no sound rent the air. Mary now ran out of the room, locking the door from the outside.

Edward read for a while longer, but soon his eyes got tired, and he laid the book down and fell asleep. He slept for a couple of hours, and when he awoke, it was dark outside. Edward had always been afraid of the dark and now more than ever. He wasn't scared of what might be floating around out there. In fact, he would welcome some otherworldly visitors about now. It was the suffocating closeness of the dark that made his skin crawl. To be closed in and cut off was the most unbearable condition he could imagine. In the past he had run away from any limiting circumstances time after time, but now he was forced to face the ultimate prison in the helpless body of a baby.

Edward cried for help and continued bawling until the door was finally opened and the lights were turned on. His father now walked over to him. He had not had an opportunity to get acquainted with Adam, or the personality he had assumed in this lifetime. In Egypt they had worked together on the pyramid of Cheops; Adam had been the chief architect and Edward was his reluctant apprentice. However, Edward was more interested in art than in building pyramids at the time. For practice he would carve naked dancers on the corner stones, which would make the priests furious. To keep him out of harm's way, Adam had extra stone blocks hauled over to a nearby cave for Edward to work on after hours.

This was considerate of him, but it was also self-serving. Adam couldn't afford to lose Edward because he needed his help on the pyramid. The project demanded more ingenuity than Adam could muster, and Edward had a genius for solving technical problems. They finally developed a good working arrangement. Edward would draw up the plans while Adam followed through on the actual construction, giving Edward more time to devote to his art. It was expedient, but it also had its negative side effects. Since that time, when they had been drawn together in other lifetimes, their relationship fell into the same pattern. Edward would supply the brain-power while Adam acted as front man.

That night, after Adam fed Edward his bottle, he carried him out to the living room to see a scale model of a building he had designed. Edward took one look at the model and started to get a headache. True to form, Adam was again determined to sidestep the laws of stress and balance. The model was beautiful. He had always been good with models, but when it came to the actual construction, his designs always fell apart. Edward crawled closer and could immediately see the structural problem. Unfortunately, Adam had unknowingly disguised the weakness so well he doubted if anybody would detect the fault before the building collapsed.

Edward was now faced with a most unwelcome dilemma. To redesign the architectural plans, if that was at all possible given his present physical limitations, would reinforce a karmic pattern that could only hinder Adam's development in the long run, not to mention his continual involvement. However, if Edward allowed Adam to go ahead with the planned building, it would no doubt collapse, possibly killing hundreds of people.

While Edward considered his options, Tolan took advantage of this grand opportunity for further moral instruction. He appeared before Edward the next day while he was lying in his crib.

"Well, Edward. I see the wheels of karma finally rolled over you," Tolan said smugly.

"Should've known you'd show up to inform me of my responsibilities to my fellow man."

"No, Edward. You have only one responsibility, here as always. And that is to yourself."

"What's the catch?" Edward asked.

"If you're true to yourself, you can't be false to any man. To paraphase my good friend, Francis Bacon."

"In other words . . ."

"You find yourself in this predicament, because in the past you took the line of least resistance. If you had been strong and not self-indulgent, Adam would never have become so dependent on you."

"Tricky. You should've been a lawyer."

"I was many times."

Edward gave this argument careful consideration. "Okay, let me get this straight. If I let Adam go through with this project, and he inadvertently kills a few hundred people, their deaths are my responsibility, because I didn't make him do his homework in the past?"

"You do catch on fast."

"Wow, and all for a little artistic freedom. What a vicious circle," Edward thought.

"No, what an opportunity for soul growth."

"I can see I don't have much of a choice then."

"On the contrary," Tolan replied, "you have free choice as always. And may that choice free you and not bind you to more pain and confusion. Till next time, peace be with you, Edward."

Tolan disappeared as Mary gingerly came into the nursery for Edward's morning feeding. The distant contemplative look on her son's face made her turn around, afraid of yet another incident. Mary walked back to the kitchen for another stiff cup of coffee.

FIVE

Edward meditated for hours on the correct course of action, until Mary caught him in the lotus position and freaked out again. Finally, he decided it was time Adam learned to fend for himself. Edward would disclose the faulty nature of this current design, and allow his father to solve the problem on his own. Hopefully, this would free him of any future entanglements. After his nap in the afternoon, Edward would crawl into his father's den, lock the door and carefully study the model. He took it apart and put it back together again a number of times until he figured out the real crux of the problem.

The stress lines of the proposed building would be entirely off center, pushing the weight distribution off to the side. Adam had ingeniously compensated for this misalignment by running a series of lateral supports back under the structure. This would throw the weight load back toward the center, which allowed the thirty-story building to rest on four corner columns. It was a futile attempt to correct one mistake with another. Edward soon discovered the weak pivot point, the focus of the weight shift, where the structure would most likely collapse. This was the corner column that held the main lateral support.

Any demonstration would have to show that the concept, not just the construction of the model, was the real culprit. Edward had to calculate the exact angle to jar the column loose so the model would collapse in the center, not just fall over on its side. With the help of a pocket calculator, he figured the angle and the exact speed needed by a projectile for the desired effect. Now how was he going to present his results?

If he gave a demonstration for Adam, he would merely repair the column and go on with the project, never suspecting that his design was at fault. At dinner several nights later, Adam solved this problem for him. He proposed throwing a party for the grand unveiling of the model, inviting his boss, the chief engineer, and the financial backers.

"You're sure this isn't too short of a notice?" Adam asked Mary.

"No, not at all. You've always said that's why you married me: for my dinner parties." Mary gave Adam a coy smile, and he looked back at her in self-satisfied appraisal.

"Doby thinks the party's a great idea. Especially the family setting. The client is a real upright, family man, patriotic type."

"I'll buy Edward a new outfit," Mary said.

"Do that." Adam sat back in his chair and lit a cigar. "Yeah, this could be my big break."

"It's about time they recognized you. You're a real genius, dear."

Adam started to blush at this description, but decided to accept the accolade in all modesty. Edward, who was lying in his playpen, put his hand to his mouth to stop from gagging, but couldn't hold back a choked-up, throaty snicker. Adam looked over at him.

"What's Edward been up to?" Adam asked.

For the last two days, Mary had seen Edward crawl into the den and close the door behind him, but after her claim of Edward's reading ability met with such derision, she wasn't about to mention this latest episode.

"Oh, nothing much. Just crawling around getting into trouble," Mary said, looking down into her cup of coffee.

Adam nodded his head, pleased with his son's manly behavior. He now stood up from the table. "Well, I think I'll give the model another coat of paint."

As Adam left the room, Edward rolled over on his side, whipped out the pocket calculator tucked away in his diaper, and figured out if the added weight of another coat would affect his calculations.

The party was held a week later. Mary went all out to set the stage for her husband's triumphant moment. After dinner everybody gathered in a circle around the draped model in the center of the living room.

"I know how excited everybody is, so I won't go into a long spiel." The others clapped in mock impatience. "I just want to say that I couldn't have come this far without the help of . . ." Adam paused, choked up with emotion, " . . . without the help of my mother, and my . . . ."

"For Christ's sake, Adam. Undrape the damn thing," Arnold Doby said, chomping down on his cigar butt.

Adam reached over and pulled the cover off the model, revealing his grand masterpiece. There were a few sincere gasps from the audience. The model itself was spectacular, and the design was fairly daring in its own right. Edward had joined the gathering for the unveiling, and he now retrieved his rubber ball from under the sofa and lined up his shot. He had a moment's hesitation, deeply regretting having to spoil such a fine evening, not to mention his father's career. And in that moment Edward experienced an emotion he had not felt in a long time, an obligation that went beyond self-interest, beyond personal or family ties, to those nameless people whose lives he was now saving.

Edward rolled his ball toward the model, hitting the column at the exact angle that slowly collapsed it from the center out. In twenty seconds it lay in shambles on the living room floor. His father nervously laughed it off, scolding Edward for making such a mess of it. Doby appeared unconcerned by the model's shoddy construction, but the chief engineer didn't take it so lightly. He saw how it fell apart at the center, and that made him uncomfortable. The whole group retired to the den and carefully went over the blueprints. Adam quickly rebuilt the model, and the engineer applying pressure on the same corner column was able to collapse the model as before. This could be corrected but the financial people wondered if anything else had been improperly designed, and if so whether they would find out about it in time to prevent a real disaster. They withdrew from the project, and Adam was fired on the spot.

Mary blamed Edward for their misfortune, and she was convinced that her son had a malevolent influence over their lives. Adam thought her suspicions were pure nonsense, but nevertheless he kept a watchful eye on Edward and was more inclined to listen to Mary's stories about his unusual behavior.

Several nights later, after Mary had retrieved what she considered conclusive evidence against her son, she again brought up the subject with her husband.

"I'm telling you, Adam. Edward is just too precocious by any standards."

"Isn't that what Dr. Peterson warned you about?"

"When she said he'd read and write at an early age, I figured three years at the outside, not six months."

Adam gave his wife a skeptical look. "So, what did you catch him reading this time, the encyclopedia?"

"He's beyond that stage," Mary said mysteriously. "Here, take a look at this." Mary handed Adam a crude drawing she had picked out of Edward's wastepaper basket.

"I'll have to admit it's pretty good, but it's not exactly a van Gogh."

"That's what I thought, until I read this month's edition of *Scientific American*, and came across what he was drawing." Mary handed her husband the opened magazine.

Adam compared his son's drawing with a picture of an alien landscape. "Now, that's scary."

"Well, that's only half of it," Mary said keeping Adam in suspense. "I picked that drawing out of his basket last week, but the magazine only came in this morning."

Adam shook his head in dismay, then turned the magazine around to read the caption. "What is it of, anyway?"

"A sunset on Mars," Mary said.

"I think Dr. Peterson has been holding out on us." Adam stood up and paced the room before deciding on a course of action. "Collect everything you find, but don't call her or say anything, not until we have a better handle on this thing."

Adam was now concerned about his son's suspicious behavior, but for the time being, he was more concerned about their dwindling bank account and his inability to find another job. This concerned Edward as well. He had chosen the Doolittles as parents because it appeared they would be able to supply him with all the comforts and luxuries of the good life. Edward had helped to dim those prospects considerably. Their future now looked bleak in comparison unless he assumed an added burden of karma and interceded on their behalf. Edward decided that life in this earthly asylum was difficult enough without adding poverty to his long list of complaints.

One afternoon Edward was lying in his crib reading a copy of *Time* magazine. He came across an article about fruit growers on the West Coast, who were forced to pay exorbitant prices to ship their produce in refrigerated freight cars across the country. The article stated that several alternative approaches for storing and shipping fresh fruits and vegetables had failed to cut costs.

Edward was surprised that an advanced civilization, which had rediscovered the principles of atomic energy, couldn't store fresh produce economically. There was a simple solution to this problem, and Adam might as well develop the pyramid storage concept before someone else did and made millions off it. Edward crawled into his father's den and left the magazine article on his desk. After dinner that night, Adam retired to the den to brood over the family's financial problems. Seeing the article, he picked up the magazine and read it. He was thoroughly unimpressed with their predicament, considering his family would soon be unable to buy their produce anyway.

That night, while Adam slept, Edward went into a deep meditation and contacted his father's subconscious mind. He implanted a dream showing fresh fruits and vegetables being loaded and shipped in pyramid-shaped containers. The locale switched to a grocery store where these vegetables were displayed and sold in miniature pyramids. Next he saw a myriad of products packaged in pyramid containers with the logo: Another Doolittle invention.

The next morning Adam woke up excited about his dream. He went to the library that afternoon and checked out several books on pyramids. A quick survey of this material revealed, as his dream had suggested, that the pyramid shape could indeed prevent rapid deterioration in matter. Adam now constructed several miniature models, and his first experiments on razor blades worked remarkably well. However, when he tried building larger models for storing produce, the results were less than satisfactory.

Adam was ready to give up on his project, when Edward interceded with another implanted dream showing these larger models aligned on a north-south axis for maximum output. This would cover stationary warehouses, but box cars would be traveling in every which direction. For them it was necessary to enclose the pyramid containers in artificial magnetic fields to simulate the proper alignment. This concept put Adam on the right track. He received a patent on his design, and after six months of documented research, he presented this project to a large growing and distribution outfit. They bought it, and in no time at all, the Doolittles were very rich.

This was more to Edward's liking. The only problem was his father's lack of generosity. Edward was no bleeding heart, but he knew that when you tapped the universal reservoir of ideas, mankind's collective inheritance, as he had for this project, you were obligated to share the advantages gained with the other heirs or incur heavy karmic backlash. To rectify this oversight, Edward would crawl into Adam's office once a week, forge his name on a check and send it off to some deserving charity. Adam didn't keep his books updated, and didn't discover these contributions until the charities began to express their gratitude, which put him in a much more generous mood.

SIX

With his parents watching more closely, Edward put on his best baby face and the next six months passed without further incident. In a few days Edward would celebrate his first birthday, and the Doolittles were throwing a party for the grand occasion. This gave them an excuse to invite Dr. Peterson to their house for questioning. She had called earlier in the year, but Mary did not tell of her suspicions. They had decided to wait until they could confront her with a solid case.

Abigail had just recently returned from Russia where she worked with a parapsychologist investigating brain wave activity in infants. His research indicated that infants register only low-frequency delta rhythms, but as their minds develop, they reach up into the theta, then the alpha and finally the beta rhythms. It was this last level of brain wave activity that showed the presence of complex thought arrangements and the development of a fully functioning human mind.

Abigail planned to pursue this line of research on her own. She hoped to discover what elements in a baby's environment stimulated higher level brain wave activity. She would then design a comprehensive program that would develop young minds faster, and hopefully far in advance of their peers. With such a program, she could create her own little cadre of child geniuses. Abigail suspected Edward was already operating at this higher level. If she could gather conclusive proof, it might be the evidence needed to coerce him into cooperating with her scheme.

From overhearing Mary talk about the party arrangements, Edward knew of Dr. Peterson's coming visit. He looked forward to seeing her again, and would use this opportunity to try out his new baby routine on a reputable expert in the field. By now Edward had done a considerable amount of research, and this latest routine had fooled parents, relatives and neighbors without exception. Of course the other babies knew, but they were in no position to tell.

The party was a huge success. Edward was in good form, spilling his beets on his new bib, dropping his bottle on the floor, and generally making a mess of it. The other babies were impressed, and following his lead they soon turned the Doolittles' kitchen into a first class pigpen. However, Abigail was somewhat less impressed with Edward's winning performance in this battle of the baby wreckers. This would be disappointing for any actor, but few of them had as much at stake as Edward. It appeared Abigail would be more formidable than he had supposed.

After the party Edward was immediately put to bed for his horrendous display of bad manners. Leaving the kitchen until morning, Mary showed Abigail to the living room where Adam joined them to discuss Edward's progress. Once they were settled, Edward slipped out of his crib and crawled over to the cracked door and listened to their discussion.

Mary told Dr. Peterson of one unexplained occurrence after another. First there was the now famous baby-reading incident at three weeks; next came the sonnet in Old English found crumpled up in Edward's wastepaper basket at three months. Adam next told the story of how Edward had wrecked a model building and showed its structural weakness at six months. Finally, Mary brought out the picture of a sunset on Mars drawn during his tooth-breaking period.

Abigail compared the drawing to the original photo and nodded her head. "Not bad. He's definitely a child prodigy." When Mary explained the week's delay between the execution of the drawing and the magazine's delivery, Abigail listened with feigned amusement. "So you're telling me Edward was reading at three weeks, writing poetry at three months, and at six months he was drawing visionary pictures of alien landscapes?" Abigail asked incredulously.

"You make it sound preposterous, but we know what we've seen," Adam insisted. "You've been holding out on us, and we want to know, deserve to know our child's real condition."

Abigail decided to lead them on with a bogus report on a recent celestial phenomenon. "You're right. There is something, but I couldn't say anything before, afraid you might read too much into innocent behavioral quirks. Earlier in the year, the northern hemisphere was bombarded by an extraordinary burst of cosmic radiation. Some children, born after the episode, have since demonstrated a wide range of developmental problems. And a few have shown precocious abilities far in advance of anything we've ever seen. Edward is one of the children we're monitoring."

The Doolittles were quite impressed by this explanation, and a little alarmed by their son's unpredictable condition. "For that reason, I have brought in an eminent Russian scientist, the one who first detected the effects of the radiation, to examine these children. With your permission, I would like him to see Edward in the morning." The Doolittles readily agreed, and Abigail would now get brain wave readings she needed to blackmail their son.

Dr. Addison had arranged for Abigail to use the hospital's facilities to run their tests. The next morning Mary brought Edward to the hospital, where Abigail introduced them to her Russian colleague, Dr. Pudunsky. Upon seeing him, Edward had a psychic flashback of the scientist in a past incarnation as an Incan witch doctor performing a sloppy brain transplant. This did not instill a high degree of confidence, and Edward would watch him very closely.

One of Abigail's assistants took Edward into the lab, where he was strapped into a harness and hooked up to an electroencephalograph. It appeared they were merely going to test his brain wave activity. Edward went into a deep meditation, and from there he was able to keep them within the delta frequency with occasional lapses into theta rhythms. A whole series of mind-expanding tests failed to alter this pattern, and Abigail was getting increasingly frustrated by the lack of results. Finally, after Edward had relaxed his defense system, she suddenly showed him a nude centerfold, and his brain waves jumped to the top of the scale.

Dr. Pudunsky had nearly fallen asleep when he detected this sudden, erratic leap on his viewing scope. This was most unusual, and he now paid closer attention to the test. Just as suddenly the beta waves ended and fell back into the lower spectrum of normal activity. It looked highly suspicious, as if the child had control over them. Vladimir found this possibility very exciting.

Irked by Abigail's trick, Edward decided to repay them in like measure. He now began to send out an erratic burst of long and short brain waves. At first neither doctor could decipher them. Vladimir, who had been a Soviet Scout as a young boy, turned up the sound, shut his eyes and listened to the beep-beep of the wave bursts. It suddenly dawned on him. The baby was sending them a message in Morse code. He quickly took out a pad of paper and began to write down the English translation of the letters:

BUG OFF LADY

Vladimir, who spoke very little English, could not understand this American slang. Abigail understood it perfectly well. She told Pudunsky it was a meaningless jumble of words, and that they were on the wrong track.

After a few more tests, which proved equally unsuccessful, they ended the session. Dr. Pudunsky left the hospital and went back to the Holiday Inn to conduct further experiments on the cocktail waitresses.

Abigail unstrapped Edward from the harness and unhooked him from the electroencephalograph. He had clearly beaten her this time, but she hadn't given up on him. One day she would gather the evidence to expose this impostor or to coerce him into working with her. Abigail now brought Edward out to his mother in the waiting room. She told Mary that their tests were inconclusive. He definitely showed signs of precocious development, but there was nothing in their results to indicate the extra-ordinary abilities suggested by her claims. Dr. Peterson urged them to continue close surveillance, and that she would return at regular intervals for further testing.

As Abigail handed Edward over to his mother, she leaned over and whispered in his ear.

"Okay, wise guy, I'm going to get you yet." Edward, his stomach upset by the long morning, responded by spitting up all over her.

SEVEN

Edward was soon able to settle into a set routine, as the Doolittles moved into a larger home in which he had his own bedroom and playroom. Mary had hired a nanny to watch him during the day, while she devoted most of her time to the many charities to which they had donated their money. Actually, she wanted to stay away from Edward as much as possible. It was flattering to have such a talented son, but it was also very disconcerting to walk into his playroom and see him repairing a television set at the ripe age of 18 months. Adam opened a firm to develop and market new inventions. The only problem was that after his initial burst of creativity, he stopped having the dreams which were the sole source of his inspiration. He became depressed, stayed home half the week, and made a general nuisance of himself. Finally, Edward was forced to give him some fresh ideas in another series of dreams. This would keep his father busy for the time being.

However, time passed slowly and a life of total confinement was boring beyond endurance. If Edward was immobilized by his physical limitations, he could always seek his freedom in that other world. He decided to check up on Rana and Cara and see how they were adjusting to life on Earth. Going into deep meditation, Edward began to read the Akashic Records (the universal memory banks) and located all his soul mates in various towns and cities around the world. Rana, who had been a male in most of his previous incarnations, had surprisingly chosen a female body this time around. Reading the records as they foretold possible future events, he could see her as a leader in the women's rights movement. And although it was obscure at this point, it appeared she could become the first woman president. Cara had chosen a female body with enormous mental capacity, and her parents were scientists working at MIT. Her future looked even more promising as the potential discoverer of the lifeforce monad and its amazing healing properties.

Most of his other soul mates chose less demanding life paths, although a few were with poor families working out their poverty cycle. Edward, who was living quite well, found this distressing. Although he respected their choices, and he didn't want to interfere with the operation of free will, Edward found it difficult to sit back and watch some of them nearly starve to death. One morning Edward slipped into his father's den and wrote off a few checks to families of some of his more indigent soul mates. He covered the money by telling them that they were winners in the National Baby Lottery.

Seeing his friends choosing such noble ambitions, or deciding to assume difficult karmic lots made Edward feel worthless. What was wrong with him? Why couldn't he commit himself to some worthwhile cause? Why did he take everything so lightly or make a joke out of even the most serious situations? He didn't feel that their crusades were hopeless, although many of them would end in apparent defeat. In the overall scheme of things, he knew every watt of energy expended in the right direction was used by forces greater than any soul, not less an individual ego, to evolve the universe into higher realms. For that reason this cosmic process had always seemed like their concern, not his. So Edward went his own way, keeping out of serious trouble, having a few laughs, but avoiding the pain and anguish such commitments seemed to bring in their wake. Yet, this rebellious course had inevitably led to a dead end.

Edward was already twenty lifetimes behind his class, and given the advantages of his present incarnation, material and transcendent, this could be a last chance lifetime for him to break out of this downward spiral or face the terrible consequences. If he didn't recover soon, he would have to answer to the "Soul Catcher," the cosmic grim reaper.

Hearing Edward give his spiritual well-being serious consideration, Tolan raced across the galaxy to be at his side, and add his opinion.

"Oh, it's you again," Edward thought, as Tolan materialized before him, embarrassed by his thoughtful reflection.

"You don't sound very happy to see me, Edward."

"How would you like somebody eavesdropping on your every thought?" Edward asked.

"If they were my Soul Guide, assigned to me for that purpose, I would welcome their contribution."

"Oh yeah, but then you wouldn't need it, because you know everything," Edward said with heavy sarcasm.

"No, Edward. You'd be surprised how much there is to learn, and how little we both know."

"Then how do you get off telling me how to run my life?"

"It's my job, and besides I've only been trying to help you clarify your thoughts and feelings," Tolan said reasonably.

"And I can just imagine your next clarification, 'Why don't you get motivated and do something?'"

"Now why would you want to do that after all this time?" Tolan asked.

"Because everybody else is committed to such fine and noble causes, while little Edward keeps fooling around."

"If you're willing to pay the price, who's stopping you?"

Edward was getting annoyed by Tolan's nonchalant attitude. "But I'm not, and I want to turn it around, but I just can't find anything worth the effort."

"Keep looking, I'm sure it'll turn up."

"And if it doesn't, who's to say it'll work out?"

"Come now, Edward. We both know it's not the results that count, but the effort," Tolan said.

"Effortless effort," Edward said, remembering an earlier lesson.

"That's right. Think about it, and the effort could bring

illumination. Until later, peace be with you, my son."

Tolan dematerialized, leaving Edward in deep thought.

EIGHT

Edward contacted several soul mates while they were dreaming, hoping that by example they might help motivate him. Unfortunately, their egos soon resented this intrusion and began to resist prolonged dream states. If allowed to continue, it could sever the connection between the ego and the Higher Self, creating an imbalance that would undermine their physical and mental well-being.

Cara, one of his more evolved soul mates, had so integrated the various levels of her being that she alone could freely communicate with Edward without fear of reprisal. The two of them spent many a day romping through the astral world, having a picnic on the astral equivalent of Parnassus or skiing down the astral Alps. However, while this connection was still so open and fluid, before time could properly ground her, Cara had to limit the outward reach of her travels. By age four she could roam the universe in her dream state, but until then she would have to stay within the earth plane, which had few of the more scenic fun spots in the galaxy.

After a few hundred trips with Edward, she became overconfident and one day went to visit her old neighborhood several light years away. At that moment Cara's mother tried to wake her and nearly severed the connection with her astral body. Cara returned in time to prevent any permanent damage, but her body consciousness, drawing on its strongest survival instincts, prevented her from taking even earthbound journeys in the near future.

"Looks like that does it, Edward."

"Let's just wait for a few months, then zip out again," Edward said.

"No, it's more serious than that. It'll take a few years to heal completely, and besides, it's time I started working on my lower self, get it ready for the job it has to do."

"So you won't have any time at all for me?"

"Now, Edward. Stop plucking those sympathy strings. I would love to be with you, but all you want to do is hang out."

"Playing can be hard work."

"Yes, but not very constructive. No, Edward. It's been fun, but right now I have to concentrate on the tasks at hand."

"Then it's goodbye?"

"Not unless you choose to work with me. How're your math skills?" Cara asked.

"No, I'd just be Edward Doolittle to you, while to me you'd be all you are. I'd find that unbearable."

"I understand. We can still meet in the spirit later, but

for now we'll have to pursue our separate destinies. Goodbye, Edward. And may the universe go with you."

After parting with Cara, Edward became depressed when he realized his absolute isolation. His soul mates were so close in physical proximity, and yet closed off to him by selfish possessive egos, they could be a million light years away. They had been together for all eternity, and would be together again in the near future, but for now they were lost to him.

If Edward was trapped down here, biding his time until that long-awaited reunion, he decided to check out the local diversions and try to keep occupied for the duration. Edward zipped around the world to see what new foolishness was afoot. He was not surprised to find a lot of old Atlantean scientists busily preparing to destroy the world again. Many of them had not incarnated since then, because the civilizations that followed did not offer the technological scope for them to work out karmic patterns. Consequently, they were relatively young souls with incredible power and knowledge, but without enough wisdom to apply it within moral guidelines. They had never really grown up, still playing with their deadly toys.

From Edward's vantage point it appeared nature might beat them to it. As he traveled through the earth's etheric currents, he could see something drastically wrong with the whole vibration of the planet. The earth's energy field, so green and vibrant in the past, had become extremely murky. Those of volcanoes and land fissures were vibrating at an incredible rate, and it was only a matter of a few years before they would tear the surface of the planet apart. He had seen it happen in the past, and in fact Edward had lived through

the Atlantean cataclysm. It was a memory of such horrendous proportions that it haunted him 12,000 years later.
He had seen the catastrophe coming and had tried to warn
the people of their impending doom, but no one would
listen. Since that lifetime, he had avoided future cataclysms
along with their burden of obligation.

Yet here he was once again stranded on a unstable
planet with no way out. Edward decided to prepare for the
worst and spent a considerable amount of time surveying
the earth's etheric field. He detected magnetic lines of force
already forming around future earthquakes and volcanic
eruptions, and using their coordinates he could chart the
coming earth changes and determine safe zones for settling.
After finding an ideal location, Edward surrounded this
property with force fields that would prevent any premature
development of the area. In time he would purchase the land
and build a survival community on the site. He planned to
contact his soul mates before the catastrophe struck and
offer them a safe place to stay.

At this point it looked like few of them would accept the
offer. Most of his soul mates were developing neglected
parts of their total being to correct past imbalances. And in
most cases, those areas did not include psychic awareness.
Edward did not want to interfere with the exercise of free
will, but he also did not want to watch their premature
demise. Assuming the responsibility, he now overrode parts
of their programming and initiated development of precog-
nitive faculties among his soul mates by directing energy
into their higher centers. When fully operative, it would
allow them to foresee enough of this impending disaster to

make the proper adjustments. This effort took time and the expenditure of enormous reserves of energy. As a consequence, it sapped Edward's personal power center and left him open to the intrusion of outside forces he normally would have been able to circumvent.

NINE

Edward spent the next few years in astral projection, watching over his property and developing his soul mates. At first Mary was delighted by Edward's inactivity, but after a while it began to worry her. Every time she peeked into his bedroom, he was sitting in the lotus position so still and lifeless that it appeared he was dead. Edward's precocious development was undeniable, but Mary wondered if it hadn't sent her son into a disturbed withdrawal from a world that offered little challenge to his superior abilities. Mary now called in Dr. Peterson for a professional opinion.

For an hour Abigail watched Edward sitting there with his eyes closed and his legs crossed. She had an idea what he was doing, but would question Mary to confirm her suspicion. Closing Edward's bedroom door, the two of them went out to the living room to discuss this latest development.

"And he's been doing this for days at a time?" Abigail asked.

"Without eating or sleeping."

"Offhand I'd say he's meditating. Are either of you into TM?"

"Not hardly," Mary said indignantly.

"I notice he's awfully skinny. Is that because he's been skipping his meals?" Abigail asked.

"That's another problem. He refuses to eat meat, and when I asked why, he said he was a vegetarian. Finally, after weeks of playing with his food, I had him draw up his own menu that included plenty of fruits and vegetables with things like yogurt and granola cereal."

"Doesn't sound very appetizing."

"That's what I thought, so when he stopped eating, I took him to our family doctor. He asked him why he'd stopped, and Edward said he was fasting for world peace. Isn't that curious?" Mary asked.

"Very. But it does fit into a pattern of sorts. I'd like to consult a colleague of mine, an Indian doctor, and see what he thinks of this three-year-old meditator."

Abigail took a picture of Edward sitting in deep meditation and sent it to Dr. Katara at the Eastern Institute for Advanced Studies. Reading the attached report, and seeing the picture of Edward in the lotus position sent Hari into samadhi. The Eastern world had been anxiously awaiting a new avatar, and an American savior could be a timely import. Katara immediately sent the picture to his master in India. Within weeks an onslaught of yogi disciples descended on the Doolittles' house to pay homage to this young American avatar.

The long-haired, disheveled pilgrims created quite a stir in the wealthy, exclusive neighborhood. They pitched their tents in the Doolittles' front yard, swam naked in their swimming pool, and chanted into the early hours of the morning. Wearing only loincloths, they went house to house begging for alms, getting doors slammed in their faces by neighbors unaware of this time-honored tradition among holy men. When they switched to selling herbal diet remedies, they received a more welcome reception.

Edward found this situation rather distressing. It not only interrupted his project, but gave Abigail more evidence to support her claim of his extraordinary development. The sooner they went back to India and forgot their newfound holy child, the sooner he could get back to work. Edward decided on a direct appeal to these sincere but gullible holy men. He called a prayer meeting for the next day at which time he would give his first public talk.

In the center of the crowded room, Edward was sitting crosslegged on a raised platform meditating. He now began to chant an ancient evocation only the most advanced of the Masters had even heard. He now opened his eyes and scanned the assembled yogis before beginning.

"Swamis, we are all aware that our brothers in the West must be freed of their material bondage, that maya has so blinded their eyes to the nature of their absolute being, that they are caught up and recklessly driven by a collective karma that threatens the very existence of life on our planet. The time is not right yet, but soon . . . very soon they will see the folly of their ways. That is why I have chosen to incarnate into an American family at this time. For by assuming the body of a Western man, I have taken on the burden of their karma. By freeing myself of it, I will open a channel into their minds and hearts. For now, you must study their language and customs, so when the time is right, you may return and show our brothers the way."

With that Edward now levitated to demonstrate his powers and to establish his right of instruction. The yogis were overwhelmed by this display and began to chant the ancient evocation. The sound vibrations sent out shook the house to its foundation, and Edward fearing its collapse around them gently returned to his mat and brought the assembled yogis to order. Before dismissing them, he wanted to impart one last message.

"My brothers, there is an American doctor who will question you about my mission. You must not reveal anything. She would use my powers to further her own crusade, a questionable venture not in harmony with the path we have chosen here today. Go in peace, and may Krishna hasten your return."

As the yogis left the prayer meeting, they silently filed past Dr. Peterson with bowed heads. The last one out was Swami Watchagucha, who had been chosen as their spokesperson. Swami was convinced that Edward was the new avatar who had come to enlighten the West, and he hoped to become the young master's campaign manager. This indolent, listless people would be no match for the wiles of a true religious adept. He could already hear the coffers filling. But first he would have to dispose of this woman doctor, who would guide Edward into less prosperous avenues.

That afternoon, while the other yogis were in their farewell meditation, Swami granted Dr. Peterson a brief interview. Wearing sunglasses, he was lying stretched out on his yoga mat by the swimming pool soaking up the rays. With Abigail's approach, Swami sat up facing the Sun while she pulled a lawn chair over and sat in his light.

After a few preliminary questions, Abigail came to the point. "Swami, I know Edward is very precocious, but are you saying he's a reincarnated master of old?"

"My good doctor, young Edward could be many things, that included, but it is much too early to tell," Swami said in precise Oxford English.

"And you have seen other children meditating at such an early age?"

"I have seen children speak foreign languages no one taught them, play musical instruments without instruction, work math problems that perplexed experts. All before the age of four."

"I have heard of such prodigies, but never believed the reports."

"They're past-life talents, residual memories, that rarely survive development of the ego in early childhood," Swami said.

"Are you saying some children do retain them?" Abigail asked.

"That depends on the talent. If it's an expression of the soul-force, a child with a strong connection can sometimes call upon it."

"What kind of talents are we talking about, Swami?" Abigail asked.

"Ones you've never read about."

"Such as?"

"I have seen children crack a bottle of formula they didn't like, slam the door in their mother's face, make a cat spin on its back."

"How is that possible?"

"Mind over matter is what created the universe to begin with. It is the pure power of the soul in activity. Some children are just more soulful than others."

Abigail could readily see the potential in this research. What if she could develop that ability in others? She could raise an army of children who would be the true masters of the universe.

"Tell me, Swami. Are there methods to help any child retain the use of such talents?" Abigail asked.

"Only a select few, but much more than would otherwise be expected."

"Why haven't you done something with this yourself?"

Swami Watchagucha carefully modulated his voice so as not to betray his greedy motives. "It would take great resources, and with no practical application, nobody has shown any interest."

"Maybe we can work something out. Show me these children."

Abigail flew to India with Swami Watchagucha, and after six months of investigation, she was convinced that the heightened development of such talents would give her children with the power and wisdom to save the world from its imminent destruction. In collusion with this renegade swami, Abigail established her own organization: the International Center for Child Resources in Houston, Texas. With the help of a dozen yogi masters, along with top scientists in the biofeedback field, Abigail began her serious research into this exciting new field.

Within a short time, working with children far less precocious than Edward, she soon realized the full extent of his extraordinary development. It was imperative that, if he continued in his obstinate refusal to work with them, his psychic talents not be allowed to flourish unchecked. She needed time to devise new ways to entrap him before he outgrew the long reach of their control. Another possibility was a development so advanced that it could successfully oppose their plans at some future date. Swami suggested that by grounding him in this world they could weaken his bond with the other, the source of his great power. Abigail visited the Doolittles and convinced them to enroll young Edward in school before his withdrawn flight from reality caused a serious emotional problem.

Mary and Adam readily agreed with this plan. They were alarmed by the recent migration of these freaky Indian yogis to their home, and their claim that Edward was an an ancient spiritual master of theirs. They were afraid some lunatic group might kidnap their son, take him to the Himalayas and make him the leader of some strange new cult. If he had ambitions in that area, as much as they disapproved, Edward should enter the seminary and become a respectable Protestant minister, not walk around in a loincloth annoying the neighbors. That September, at the tender age of four, Edward began his illustrious grammar school career.

TEN

Mary and Adam sat across the desk from Mr. Crenshaw, the principal of Tyler Elementary. Malcolm was thumbing through Edward's tests, impressed with the high scores. Every year some eager parent would parade the latest preschool genius past him in hopes of unloading their problem child ahead of time. Usually the tests revealed aptitude, but here was a four-year-old who knew arithmetic. Malcolm looked up at the anxious parents.

"This is highly irregular. As a rule, we never accept children before the legal age."

"I understand. But I think my son warrants special consideration," Adam insisted.

"My dear sir, if you only knew how many preschool wonders I've seen in my day."

"But how many could read, write, and...do algebra?"

"Among other things," Mary added, drawing a disapproving scowl from her husband.

Crenshaw looked down at the test papers. Edward had been given a comprehensive grammar school placement test; who would have thought to include high school subjects? Maybe this child did deserve special consideration.

Malcolm glanced over at Edward sitting on the sofa in his preschool genius outfit: brown corduroy suit with elbow patches, horn-rimmed glasses, and parted slicked-down hair. "Young man, I'm going to make an exception in your case, and allow you to enroll in our fine school. Now we maintain high academic standards, enforce strict discipline, and expect our students to conduct themselves accordingly." Malcolm gave Edward a stern intimidating look. "I hope you won't disappoint me."

"I'll try my best, sir," Edward said, while planning a program of underachievement that would impress all concerned.

Edward was finally placed in the fourth grade. His classmates were fairly conscientious, but he was far too advanced to have any intellectual interests in common with them. Classroom instruction proved to be boring, and so Edward decided to get a head start on life by researching future career opportunities. He went to the library in town, and with his father's card he checked out books on electrical and aeronautical engineering. With the petroleum-based energy supply running down, he knew the Western world would soon consider solar energy as a feasible alternative. This could be a great opportunity for him. Every day during class Edward worked on a preliminary design for a solar crystal reactor, similar to the ones used in Atlantis to convert the sun's rays to electrical energy. He hid the sketches under his school work, pulled them out whenever he could, and by the end of the first semester had finished a prototype design worth a small fortune.

Another prospect was the space industry, which had been virtually closed down in the early seventies after the last manned space flight. For future exploration they would need a less expensive and more streamlined propulsion system than fuel-guzzling rocket engines. There was an easier, economical method for traveling in space, as well as within the earth's atmosphere. Edward spent the second semester designing an anti-gravity device that reversed electrical and magnetic forces. In an airplane it repelled the earth's magnetic lines of force to push the craft forward. In space it reversed the gravitational pull of stars and large planets to propel a spacecraft at great speeds. With such vehicles the Atlanteans had explored the distant reaches of our solar system, and later used the device to build the great pyramids of Egypt.

There was one major obstacle to the development of such new age technology. These miraculous new inventions would have to be an extension of earlier work in both fields to avoid the type of suspicion that could lead to Edward's exposure, even if he again used his father as front man. He had hoped that, with all these Atlantean scientists coming in at this time, someone with a touch of genius had stumbled on even the most elementary equations. It wouldn't take much background work for him to base his theories on and build his devices. Unfortunately, it would be another fifty years before science began to readjust its thinking and seriously explore these new areas.

Miss Mumford, Edward's fourth grade teacher, seeing her industrious student make only average grades, told his parents at their first PTA meeting that Edward was doing fine considering his age, but he was definitely no genius. This was encouraging news, but they would await Dr. Peterson's assessment before celebrating. Soon after, Edward's grades began to drop when he gave up hope of ever presenting his able inventions. He now looked into other career opportunities, but couldn't turn up anything that remotely interested him. With his experience he could succeed at anything. In fact, there were talents like painting, highly developed in past lifetimes, that he could now use at the same level of proficiency. And yet every possibility just seemed to add more energy to the world's collective insanity.

Finally, Edward found a career that did not contribute to the present downward spiral. He decided to become a clown when he grew up, or grew out of his miniature body. He would drop out of school, run away from home and join the circus. Here, in the garb of a clown, he might be able to reach people by poking fun at their foibles. Before moving on to the big top, Edward needed to hone his talents and update a routine last used as court jester for King Henry VIII.

His first target was Miss Mumford. What annoyed Edward more than anything was how she chose to impart her great fund of knowledge by pounding it into their heads. His days were crammed with one senseless drill after another, going over the same thing repeatedly. These oral recitations didn't satisfy her, because every half hour she would go to the blackboard and write out the lessons for them to copy. Before long Edward got tired of this routine. One day, when the plumbers were working on the heating system, he followed behind them and installed a series of air jets along the base of the blackboard. While Miss Mumford was writing out another dreary lesson the next day, Edward threw the compression switch under his desk, and the air jets blew her dress up over her head. She continued writing while trying to pull the dress down as her students laughed at this comical juggling act. Finally, she turned away from the blackboard and resumed their oral recitations. In the next week, after this scene was repeated several times, Miss Mumford became so disconcerted she gave up on drilling them either way.

Another annoying practice was the strict regimen the school ran on. Every forty-five minutes the bell rang and they switched subjects. This stifled the whole creative flow of their learning experience, and interrupted Edward's ongoing design work. Finally, he snuck into the principal's office and fixed the electrical device that triggered the bell. The next day the bell was out of order, and their class settled into a more natural rhythm that sparked new enthusiasm in his classmates. Mr. Crenshaw brought in an electrician to fix the device, but Edward kept shorting out the main circuit with a couple of psychic jabs. By the third day, and several electricians later, Crenshaw gave up on his precious system and allowed his teachers to set their own time periods.

As a result there were now longer recess and lunch periods. This allowed Edward more time to polish a magic act he would need later when he joined up with the circus. He now began to practice on his classmates, and pretty soon this act drew large crowds after lunch every day in the playground. Actually, there wasn't very much real magic involved. Edward had never been very good with the standard sleight-of-the-hand tricks. He relied more on his psychic powers to bend forks with his mind, materialize rabbits in clear fishbowls or a snake in a teacher's bouffant hairdo. Mr. Crenshaw, seeing the publicity value in young Edward's magic act, booked him in grade schools across the city. Before long his popularity spread, and Edward was asked to perform at charitable functions in the area culminating in his appearance at the annual March-of-Dimes Telethon.

Mr. Crenshaw had bargained with Edward's services to have himself hired as M.C., and negotiated appearances by several other young performers. Now Malcolm watched in horror as his juggler dropped one ball after another. Finally, Crenshaw walked out on the stage to stop the performance.

"Not bad, Mark. We're just glad they weren't hand grenades," Malcolm said, drawing a few laughs from the adults present. Mark gathered up his props and walked off the stage. "Now the act everybody has been waiting for. Let's hope that Edward Doolittle gives us more than just a little magic."

Edward now walked out onto the stage dressed in his undersized tuxedo. The students in the audience gave him a rousing ovation. Edward now took off his top hat and handed it to Mr. Crenshaw.

"Sir, if you will inspect my hat," Edward said.

Malcolm looked inside, and using the fingers on his raised hand, counted off what he imagined seeing. "Well, outside of a dozen rabbits, four pigeons, and two white mice, there's nothing in it." This drew more laughter from the adult contingent.

"Then you won't mind trying it on for size?" Edward asked.

Mr. Crenshaw took up the challenge and placed it on his bald head. Edward waved his wand several times, and taking this as his cue, Malcolm removed the hat. There were two fried eggs cooking on his head. Edward snapped his wand once, and the egg yolks burst and ran down Crenshaw's face. The students applauded this trick, while some of the adults booed their displeasure. Malcolm hurried off the stage wiping his face dry.

Edward went on to give one of his best performances, astounding the local television audience with his amazing feats of magic. For the climax of his show, a shower curtain was rolled out onto the stage. Edward had devised a grand finale that required two special assistants.

"If Mr. and Mrs. Crenshaw will now step forward," Edward said.

They walked out to center stage. Malcolm took Edward's microphone and called out to his supporters. "I hope Edward can turn me into school superintendent."

"If you'll please step behind the curtain," Edward said. With them in place, he pulled the curtain shut, waved his wand several times, and then opened it. The Crenshaws were standing there in their underwear.

Malcolm and his wife, seeing their scanty attire, rushed off stage. Two strong-armed gym teachers came out and dragged Edward away, while the students in the audience stomped their feet calling for Edward's return. To prevent a riot, he was allowed a curtain call during the final commercial break that ended the telethon.

This brought an end to Edward's short but highly entertaining career as an amateur magician. However, Edward soon became a folk hero among children across the city as the one child who had defied the adults and finally put them in their place. Pretty soon there were Edward Doolittle fan clubs, T-shirts with a picture of his sneering face; and a poster, showing Edward pulling back the curtain to reveal the Crenshaws, became a best-seller in the kiddie culture. In the months that followed, there were a rash of pranks perpetrated against symbols of adult pomposity. One minister went through an entire service with one of Edward's posters stuck to his bottom side. At city council the mayor was signing a bill cutting school appropriations, when a picture of Edward popped out of the pen's top. It then exploded, splattering ink on the council members.

Edward was blamed for these pranks, and placed under constant surveillance by the school authorities, which only allowed the real culprits more freedom for further mischief. This made life somewhat unpleasant for Edward, but not nearly as much as his new role as a child celebrity. There were autograph parties for his recently penned biography, guest appearances at local dances and private slumber parties. Finally, he was forced to hire a secretary to handle the fan mail, and turn down all the invitations. At the peak of this attention, when his life was a series of mob scenes, Dr. Peterson stepped in and offered Edward a way out of his pre-dicament. She was in this part of the country on a six-week recruiting tour in search of new candidates for her psychic development program. Before returning to Houston, Abigail dropped in on the Doolittles to check Edward's progress.

After Mary played a video tape of Edward's command performance at the telethon, and updated her on his new notoriety, Abigail was more convinced than ever that he was the child to lead her army of children. She was absolutely amazed by the range of his psychic abilities; he was considerably more advanced than any of her yogi hirelings. With his support they could probably accelerate their development program by leaps and bounds. Edward's charisma, which had already attracted a large following, would be another asset to their movement. With Edward as their leader, these children would march into hell after him. Abigail decided to make him another offer. If Edward refused to cooperate, he wouldn't get off as lightly this time.

Mr. Crenshaw had lent Abigail his office for the interview in hopes that Edward would accept her scholarship offer. Edward now came in and sat down across the desk from her.

"Well, Edward. How have you been?" Abigail asked.

"Taking it easy."

"Oh, really. From what I hear, you've been getting into a little trouble lately."

"Seem to have a knack for that," Edward said.

"I would agree. Yes, most definitely," Abigail said. "But it's not your only talent, now is it?"

"I spin a mean yo-yo," Edward replied.

"There's no use playing games with me, Edward. I know just how developed you are."

"And just how developed would that be?"

"For starters, you remember your past lives. More important, your psychic talents have remained intact. You're clairvoyant, telepathic and probably have certain telekinetic powers," Abigail said triumphantly.

"I see you took in my show."

"Quite a performance. It was a shame to waste it on such a small audience."

"You would book me in larger auditoriums?" Edward asked.

"With me the world would be your audience."

Edward closed his eyes and tuned into a possible alternative future if he decided to cooperate with her movement. Abigail could almost touch the reality of this vision, and it thrilled her. Edward pulled back from this nightmare in disgust.

"Think I'll pass on it," Edward said.

"Fortunately, in the last year I've discovered other children with your abilities, and so your cooperation is not critical."

"That's a relief," Edward said sarcastically.

"No, it's your loss. It won't be long before we assert our influence in the political arena, and as our star rises yours will fall."

"What's your first performance: Macbeth?"

"Not quite, because we have the witches on our side," Abigail said.

"Peterson, when are you going to grow up? You can't use these forces for selfish purposes and get away with it."

"That's religious superstition. Like electricity, it's a force of nature subject to those who can utilize the energy," Abigail insisted.

"We'll see," Edward replied.

Abigail was disappointed in Edward's continued refusal to join her movement. Although his participation was no longer crucial, she had a brief glimpse of that glorious future with Edward as their leader, and she would pursue that dream for now. However, seeing a demonstration of his great powers, she had to be certain they weren't turned against her at some later date. When Abigail returned to Houston, she dispatched her best agent to maintain a close surveillance of Edward's activities and report back to her. With one false move, she would have him captured and put in cold storage.

PART TWO

ELEVEN

Edward's highest ambition had been merely to pass a little time, have a few laughs, and exit from this backward planet for good. Unfortunately, he had brought in along with his elevated awareness the accumulated karma of fifty lifetimes. Every thought, every action sprang from bedrock strata buried deep within him. If he felt victimized by present circumstances, he could only change the outward pattern of his life by altering that hidden inner design.

It was high time Edward dealt with those past mistakes, corrected those archaic attitudes that continued to bring more pain and confusion into his present life. Edward decided to swallow his pride and ask Tolan for some much-needed advice. His mentor was only too happy to oblige him.

"Hey, Tolan. You there?" Edward thought.

"Right here," Tolan said, as he suddenly materialized

in Edward's back yard.

"That was fast."

"I pride myself on quick, friendly service." Tolan was evidently pleased by the nature of this long-awaited summons.

"Let's hope you can get me out of this mess just as quickly."

"So it's getting just a little confusing, is it?"

"Yeah, it's been one big joke."

"You're not laughing, Edward."

"I keep missing the punch line," Edward said, "but not the punch."

"And you thought by staying in your shell you could avoid any hard knocks?"

"Let's say I haven't been looking for any trouble."

"It just found you, is that it?" Tolan asked.

"Yeah, in a manner of speaking."

"Edward, with your dubious past, you'd run into trouble living on a mountain top."

"Okay, you're right," Edward said. "So where do we go from here?"

"Well, we could review your past lives and see how these patterns have slowly evolved. But, for heady people like you, more knowledge often adds only more confusion."

"Yeah, I'm a living example of that," Edward said.

"It would be better if you start by working with your soul mates. They're an extension of you, that's why you're connected, and you will be able to see yourself in them more clearly."

"But they're so gung ho, so concerned about helping

others, while I've only been hanging out looking for a good time."

"That hasn't always been the case, now has it?" Tolan asked. "Somewhere along the line you were hurt, and are hiding this sore spot with a cynical attitude."

Edward looked away, sensing the truth in this observation. "Could be, and I'll give it a try...but don't expect too much."

"And don't you accept too little," Tolan replied. "Peace be with you, Edward. And when you need my counsel, just call on me."

After Tolan's visit Edward dedicated himself to this quest. He would unlock the secret to his past through his deep connection with his soul mates, and hopefully break out of this self-defeating pattern and free himself at last. Edward decided to run away from home, but he didn't want every policeman in the country looking for him. He wrote a short letter to Dr. Peterson telling her his plans, and warning her it would be useless to alert the police or hire a private detective to track him. He would teleport himself from place to place leaving no trace behind, and it would appear to the uninformed that he simply vanished into thin air. What Edward did not realize was that Abigail's child psychics also had this ability, and that he was already being shadowed by a master of it. When Abigail received the letter, she called the Doolittles, who were not overly concerned about their son's disappearance. She told them not to worry, that she would find Edward and bring him back home. They told Abigail to take her time.

Edward's first stop was Boston where Cara, who was

now Carol Porter, was living and going to school. He needed a tight cover that would allow close contact with Carol over a long period. Edward decided to apply for a teaching position at her private school. He went out and bought grey hair color to tint his hair, makeup to apply a few wrinkles, and several sets of grownup clothes to wear. In this disguise he would easily pass as a middle-aged midget. Next he typed up a resume using a series of modern teaching positions that best reflected his experience from past lives.

After a successful interview, Edward was hired as the school's new history teacher. It was easy to fool the other teachers, but his students detected something odd about Edward. He was just too smart to be a teacher. They figured he was a bright student from another school district, placed in this position because of the shortage of teachers during their annual strike for higher wages. They found him much more knowledgeable, but it was Edward's offbeat approach to history that sparked new interest in this normally dry subject. His students loved to hear his crazy stories about the historical figures they studied. Edward made these characters come alive, sketching portraits of flesh-and-blood people with shortcomings similar to those of their parents.

After the first semester, Edward's class received the school's highest marks on a comprehensive nationwide exam on world history. They now placed him in charge of Carol's class of advanced students. This was exactly how Edward had planned it. However, he now found it difficult to teach with Carol staring back at him from the second row. Edward kept getting flashbacks of her in one of their many past lives together. One day she was Sonta, the Egyptian princess, and he was Rajai, the temple priest, whose illicit love had caused his banishment from the kingdom. Another day she was the mistress of King Henry VIII, and he was the court jester, whose wicked puns about the king's love life had cost him his tongue.

Edward began to fall in love with Cara all over again. When he pressed to get closer, arranging private work sessions after school, he soon realized to his great disappointment that she had become an obnoxious little brat. No memories from the past could soften the irritating effect of her close presence. She had never been overly affectionate in any of her past lives, always regal and distant with her cute roman nose pointed in the air. Now her soul forces had completely subdued all forms of social interest or personal empathy, and had concentrated on developing an acute intelligence. For years Edward had tried to awaken her latent psychic abilities, and if he had been successful they could have communicated at this level, but he was forced to stop because it created such a violent conflict with her present personality makeup. If Edward was going to reach her, he would have to try another approach.

Carol found most of her classes boring, and she spent her time in class solving calculus problems or drawing models of DNA molecules. To her surprise, she found Edward's history class fascinating. This disturbed her. Carol considered history a frivolous subject, and she was curious about a presentation that made it appear even remotely interesting. In the lunch room one day, she sat next to Edward to question him about his novel approach.

"Tell me, Mr. Doolittle. Why would a man of your

evident intelligence want to spend his life thinking about the past?"

"That could prove boring, if it wasn't the future I was actually studying," Edward said.

"I don't believe I understand you."

"What if time is in fact multi-dimensional and not linear as we now suppose?" As Edward had expected, this abstract concept engaged Carol's higher mental faculties. "And our passage through time is like playing three-dimensional chess: movement at different levels all happening simultaneously?"

"Then some past move could be determined by a future move, and one in the present could affect both of them," Carol said.

"Precisely, my dear."

"That's an interesting concept, Mr. Doolittle. What do you see as its practical application, if I may ask?"

"Such a concept, if acted upon, would free us and give us complete control over our destiny...undoing the past... re-ordering the future...all by our present actions."

"Here, let me see what I can do with it."

Carol pulled out a notebook and began to write out several lines of mathematical equations. Edward had hoped that this high level of abstract thinking would induce, as it had for many down through the ages, a state of cosmic consciousness. Unfortunately, her mind could not make a leap into such a brave unknown at this time. Carol was locked into a set pattern, and Edward could not interfere wthout creating conflicts he had no right to impose merely to satisfy his own yearning for companionship.

"By my calculations a free-floating body, outside any

large gravitational fields...and traveling at the speed of light, might experience time distortions of this magnitude, but no earthbound body could."

"Our bodies may indeed be earthbound and subject to gravity, but could there be other parts of us freed from the tyranny of matter?" Edward asked a puzzled Carol, who went off to think about it.

Edward was heartbroken. To be so close to her and yet so far away was unbearable for him. She had loved him through eternity, and yet was unable to respond to him now when he needed her the most. He would not interfere with her destiny and with the great contribution she could make to mankind. Carol was slated to discover the lifeforce monad in one possible future.

Edward would free her, and in doing so would free himself as well. He was learning about self-interest and personal attachment, a much neglected lesson overlooked in the past. There were more important prerogatives than personal well-being, fame, fortune and love, especially now in this most crucial period. Edward was beginning to understand the needs of the "other," as opposed to those of the self.

TWELVE

Halfway through the second semester, Edward noticed a very unusual student in his class. What brought the young boy to his attention were his consistently average test scores. If they were perfect, he could have dismissed him as being very bright, but he always received the same mark, an intermediate 85. Edward tried to check his records, but he wasn't registered at the school. The other students didn't know him, and he only attended Edward's first class in the morning and last one in the afternoon, disappearing between times. Edward trailed him to the basement one day, but when he went inside, the boy had vanished into thin air.

Edward suspected the worst several days later when he spotted Peter following him after school. The next morning he was eating breakfast in the same restaurant, and that night Peter attended the same movie. To test his range,

Edward took a shuttle flight to New York that weekend. When he failed to make the flight, Edward figured he had lost him, but Peter was waiting for him at the airport. As planned he teleported back to Boston, and when Peter lost his trail and showed up at school several days later looking for him, Edward knew the limits to the young spy's powers. With his escape assured, he decided to confront him and hopefully discover his exact orders. They met at an ice cream parlor across the street from the school.

Edward hopped up onto the bar stool, while Peter sipped his strawberry milkshake. "Okay, Peter, you're either working for the FBI or Abigail Peterson. And one's worse than the other."

"What gave me away?" Peter asked, surprised by his discovery.

"Your disappearing act was suspicious, but it was your reappearing act that clinched it."

"I thought I did that very well."

"You did, and I'm sure you're a credit to the whole program, but you're still new at this, aren't you?"

"I've put in my time," Peter said, slurping up the bottom of his milkshake.

"Well, you're certainly wasting mine." Edward reached over and zapped Peter into full attention. "Now tell me, what were your orders?"

"To maintain a close surveillance, and keep you out of harm's way."

"Just what I need: a guardian angel," Edward said sarcastically.

"You could think of me in that way."

"The only way I want to think of you, is gone."

"I'm sorry, and I know how much stronger you are," Peter said, rubbing his arm sore from Edward's electrified punch, "but I've got my orders."

Edward did not like the fanatical zeal of this young soldier, but felt confident that he could easily outmaneuver him. "Follow them, but you'll never catch up with me."

He could have pulled a few more psychic punches on Peter to stall any pursuit, but knew the karma attached to such attacks and chose not to add to his already substantial backlog. Edward finally decided that if Peter wanted to chase after him, let him burn up his energy.

It was now time to leave Carol and allow her to pursue her separate destiny. Edward's farewell was little more than a halfhearted wave across a crowded lunch room to a preoccupied little brat in pigtails. That afternoon he handed in his resignation, and took off on the next leg of his journey. After a series of evasive maneuvers, he arrived in Chicago where Rana, who was now Renee Stewart, resided.

Edward's relationship with Rana had always been that of a strong masculine friendship, but then he had never known him as a woman. Rana had chosen the body of a woman with its built-in emotional and intuitive tendencies to correct the imbalance of cold, aggressive traits from a long string of male incarnations. After a period of assimilation, she had planned to move into a man's world of business and politics to break down barriers that impeded mutual respect and cooperation among the now opposing sexes.

The next day Edward enrolled in school and was placed in Renee's sixth grade class. He didn't know what to expect, but just seeing Rana in a skirt would be well worth the long trip. Unfortunately, Renee only wore jeans to school. From the first day she took an instant dislike of Edward, and would stare at him from the back of the room. He tried to avoid her, but during the change of class, Renee kept stepping in his way until Edward was forced to push her aside. She took offense. Nobody had ever stood up to her, and Renee immediately recognized a threat to her position as class bully. After school, with her classmates watching, she walked up to Edward in the playground and slugged him in the stomach. He took her best shot without flinching, and then grabbed Renee by the arm and threw her over his back onto the ground. She lay there in total shock for a moment before she began to cry. Edward helped her up, brushed off her dirty jeans, and walked her to the bus.

The next day Renee came to school wearing a dress. She was now hopelessly in love with Edward, and she was determined to press her affection on him at all cost. Renee sat next to him in each of their classes, blinking her eyes and blowing kisses at him. In the hallway she would bump into him, at lunch sit next to him, and after school ask to carry his books home each day. The other girls, who found Edward attractive, knew to stay away. One brazen young girl didn't heed the warning signs, and tried to dance with Edward at a Saturday night sock-hop, only to have Renee drag her off the floor by the hair of her head.

Edward would have been flattered by the young girl's ardent show of affection, if he didn't see Rana's manly features behind each coquettish look. It was time Edward explained to Renee the nature of their friendship. That afternoon Edward finally let her carry his books home while they talked.

"Look, Renee," Edward said, as they walked down the tree-lined boulevard. "You don't really love me. What you're feeling is a bond of friendship from our past lives together."

"Oh, so we've been together before. How romantic."

"As pals, not lovers, and this time you're just confusing the two."

Renee walked on, trying hard to understand. "But, if I was a man then, and I'm a woman now, wouldn't that change things?"

"For you, since you don't remember, it does. But, for me, since I do remember, nothing has changed," Edward said.

"You just have to learn to live in the present, that's all," Renee said, as she took Edward's arm and snuggled up to him.

Renee was right in one regard. Her present definitely took precedence over his past. If Edward rejected her now, he might stunt the struggling emergence of her feminine tendencies. That development, not only for her soul growth but for her coming contribution to mankind, demanded his attention. Edward had come in search of an old camaraderie to quicken his lagging spirits, but found instead an old drinking buddy in need of dancing lessons.

It was to be a novel revival of Shaw's *Pygmalion*, with Edward playing Professor Higgins to Renee's Eliza. The first order of business was a new wardrobe, replacing blue jeans with dresses and T-shirts with halter tops. Next came a stylish new hairdo, makeup to soften hard features, followed by lipstick and nail polish. With enough artistry you could remake the physical appearance, but an emotional bias was somewhat harder to reorient. It took Edward longer to teach Renee to walk like a lady and not a lumberjack, to sip her tea and not guzzle it down, to eat one morsel at a time and not stuff her face. In the end, to speed up the process, he did a psychic lobotomy on her. And, within six months, his program had turned Renee from a tomboy into a lovely young lady with boys lined up asking her to dances instead of to football games.

Edward had answered the call to a higher priority than his own selfish need for companionship with an old friend. It had given him an opportunity to apply his knowledge and use his powers for a worthwhile project, and he had not done that for ages. It was the misuse of the frivolous use of that knowledge and those powers that had led to his present state of confusion. To gain a clearer understanding of his own individual destiny, Edward would next confront a soul mate who had lost his way and was in need of direction.

Edward spent another three months with Renee overseeing her development, but by now she had integrated enough of her female side to complete her mission. After school let out for the summer and he had parted with Renee, Edward wished he were home with his parents enjoying a carefree vacation. His childhood had been stolen from him along with the youthful enthusiasm of one who had all his discoveries before him. It was no fun being six going on six thousand as the burden of his selfhood weighed heavily on him. Edward was paying for all those frivolous lifetimes, for all those neglected responsibilities. However, freedom did not lie in the past but in the present, and it was time for him to move on.

THIRTEEN

When Peter showed up in Chicago, Edward had already left. He was having trouble following Edward's astral trail as he zipped from one location to the next. Traveling at such speeds caused a disturbance similar to a sonic boom, and left an impression on the etheric web surrounding the Earth. However, strong emotions directed from one person to another left trace markings that could obscure these streaks. Checking such leads proved tiresome, if not at times amusing. However, Peter now had a fresh trail to follow and took off after Edward in hot pursuit.

Edward had traveled to San Francisco in search of Robarte, who was now Bobby Davis. He had run away from home at the age of eight and lived in the Haight-Ashbury district. Bobby survived by panhandling for loose change during the day and washing woks in a Chinese restaurant at night. Once again he was caught up in the downtrodden pattern of his last twenty lifetimes. And yet before his Atlantean incarnation, Robarte had been a shining light for all the world to behold. Some devastating moral setback, during this crucial period, had maimed his spirit and sent him into a tailspin for 12,000 years.

Edward followed Bobby to his favorite corner the next morning where he panhandled businessmen and secretaries on their way to work. By noon he had collected enough money for that day's supply of drugs. Apparently it was his daily routine. From a distance Edward was able to inspect the young derelict's astral body and detected considerable damage from drug abuse. If continued it would deplete his vital energy and diminish his ability in future lives to pull out of this downward spiral. Of course, given infinite time, Robarte's prospects for recovery were good. Yet, when you added twenty wasted lives of pain and anguish to a hundred that might follow, the toll exacted made salvation's vaunted rewards sound hollow in comparison.

Seeing Bobby's condition and watching him bury himself deeper moved Edward greatly. He was determined to intercede on his friend's behalf. In his new street clothes, Edward moved out into the district and took up the life of a young beggar. It wasn't long before he had struck up a friendship with Bobby. At lunch every day, Edward would eat a large vegetarian plate at the local health food restaurant while Bobby waited for him, smoking a joint. In time he began to listen to his new friend's rap on drugs, and soon he was making efforts to free himself of this dependency.

When Bobby joined him for lunch, Edward would

prepare a special mega-vitamin dressing designed to balance
the glandular system and eliminate toxins from the body. It
wasn't long before Bobby was strong enough to withstand
the next phase of his rehabilitation. One night, while they
were staying in an abandoned warehouse, Edward placed
Bobby under hypnosis and regressed him back to his Atlantean incarnation, calling up soul records from that trouble-
some time where many of his current problems began.

It was during the bleak period when the last of Atlantis
was torn apart by earthquakes and tidal waves. Bobby, who
was then Rote, a temple priest, had earlier warned his people
of their impending doom and implored them to put aside
their material ways and turn back to their spiritual nature.
Most of his followers did not heed this warning, including
his brothers and sisters, who were among those lost in the
final cataclysm. Rote had blamed himself for their deaths. In
despair he denied his beliefs by taking his own life. For the
next twenty lifetimes, he had carried the burden and the
pattern of that guilt. It was an acid eating away at his soul
and drying up one lifetime after another.

Under Edward's guidance, during several long sessions,
Bobby relived those events and gradually released the pent-
up psychic energy in his astral body. This awakened soul
forces held in check by a massive emotional block and
allowed them to begin the long healing process. It would
take time, but Bobby had taken the first step by forgiving
himself. He had been subconsciously drawn to California, as
he was to other geologically unstable areas in the past,
because of an upcoming earthquake. Bobby had forced
himself to relive that ancient cataclysm over and over again,

in other places and in other times, as further punishment for his sins. Edward now gave Bobby a book about the Great California Quake, in hopes that he would meet this disaster in a more positive manner. Before long Bobby had started an underground railroad to move homeless street children out of the danger zone and place them back East.

Edward had been with Bobby in Atlantis. He too had tried to warn the people of the impending disaster, and when they refused to listen and were destroyed, Edward became disheartened. Although he did not fall into deep despair, which had driven Rote to suicide, Edward's response proved just as devastating. He became bitter and cynical and died a lonely, half-crazed recluse. After that period, in future lifetimes on Earth, Edward had disavowed any further responsibility toward the rest of mankind. His stumbling block was the belief that because his noble efforts proved futile, it was useless to try again. So he waltzed through future incarnations, avoiding commitments and for the most part leaving his many lives unlived.

Edward sensed that his present cycle of soul growth was complete. With his backlog, he suspected there were more challenges to meet before he cleaned his slate clear. He could wait for them to appear, unsure of which to choose, or he could ask Tolan for advice.

"Personally," Tolan said as Edward rowed the canoe across the lake, "I think you should go for a home run."

"But that's not your 'official' opinion?"

"No, the book says, 'Do it slow and do it right,' but we both know how impatient you are."

"Agreed."

"And besides, you're so far behind it might be the only way to beat the old 'Soul Catcher.'"

"That guy still hanging around?" Edward asked with alarm.

"He's made inquiries."

"But I've been making such great progress lately."

"You know they're only concerned with the bottom line, and you've been in the red for ages."

"Well, he'll never get me."

"If I were you, I wouldn't rest on my laurels," Tolan said with some concern.

"Okay, what's that home run you're talking about?"

"Dr. Peterson's movement."

"What do I need to do?" Edward asked. "Stop them, or what?"

"You need to turn your stumbling blocks into stepping-stones," Tolan said.

FOURTEEN

After Edward's talk with Tolan, while he was wondering how to approach Dr. Peterson, he took a sightseeing tour of San Francisco. At the end of the day, he was riding a cable car when a young boy took the seat next to him. It was Peter.

"That was quite a move you pulled on me back in Boston," Peter said.

Edward smiled. He was beginning to like this young spy. "Just a little trick I picked up in the Orient."

"I'd love to learn it."

"So you could follow me even closer?" Edward asked.

"It would make my job a lot easier."

"Tell you what. I'll do it real slow this time, and you see if you can keep up."

Edward stepped off the cable car, walked down a deserted alley and zipped away. Peter followed after him. In real time it took less than a second to teleport down to Abigail's research center in Houston, but for Peter the trip was much slower. Finally, half an hour later, while Edward sat on a park bench feeding pigeons, Peter materialized with a static charge that fried several birds.

"Do you always show up in a puff of smoke?" Edward asked, as burnt feathers floated down around him.

"Sorry, got my wires crossed."

"And you want to follow closer," Edward said. "Forget it."

They were in the park across the street from the Center for Child Resources. Peter realized, without having to ask, that Edward had chosen this destination to check out their program.

"Well, shall we go," Peter said. Edward nodded his head and the two of them walked across the street to the institute.

Edward was given an introductory tour and treated as a potential candidate for their development program. That day there were fifty young children going through an intensive screening process. Dr. Pudunsky was head of the testing program, and when he was introduced to Edward, he remembered him well.

"Ah yes, you were the first child tested. Got away, didn't you. You wouldn't today," Pudunsky said, looking down the row of computerized, biofeedback monitors. He now threw his head back and laughed.

The shrill high pitch of his mad laughter brought the quiet laboratory to a complete stop, as several monitors flashed warning signals questioning this candidate's suitability. The laughter sent a chill down Edward's spine, and he seriously doubted if the scientist could pass his own entrance exam. That afternoon, watching the sophisticated testing procedure, Edward had to agree with Pudunsky that it would indeed be difficult for him to fool them now.

The next morning Edward was turned over to Swami Watchagucha, who conducted the training program for all new recruits. In the gymnasium Edward saw a long line of students practicing hatha yoga exercises. Twisting and turning their bodies, they were harnessing every volt of available energy for mind control. In the raja yoga class, students using biofeedback monitors lowered their brain wave rhythms and began to tap a universal source of energy utilized by few people in the past.

The next stage of their training dealt with the practical application of this newly released energy. Here the students, under Swami's instruction, raised the energy up their spines and burst open their higher psychic centers. In an advanced class, Edward watched a row of children facing each other and using their heightened faculties to read minds, send thoughts or receive them. Next came instructions on how to impress thoughts on an unsuspecting victim until the target could not distinguish between an original and a transplanted thought. The final exercise utilized a potent form of thought transference to control a person's will and direct their actions.

With Abigail's security clearance, Edward attended the center's most advanced training sessions that afternoon. Here Swami conducted mind-over-matter exercises. At first the students merely bent forks and flipped coins, but after this preliminary warm-up, they worked their way up to moving a massive five-ton steel ball. Earlier that semester, an excited recruit had lost control and sent the ball rolling through the side wall into the parking lot. Next came mind-over-gravity lessons. Sitting in the lotus position, the students formed a circle around Swami in the center. Watchagucha slowly levitated above his mat, and the others straining from the exertion rose hesitantly into the air. Swami had once tried a double flip and a tuck from this position but fell to the floor and broke his little toe.

Further exercises were conducted outside. Using the duck pond, the students learned how to walk on water or, if they failed, how to walk on the bottom of a pond. Walking up the side of a building or through steel walls proved more difficult and more costly for those who fell short. In the day's final exercise, a group of advanced students would reduce their physical bodies to a thought vibration and teleport to a predetermined destination. Swami once again led the formation as they zipped out of sight. Edward was told that on a similar exercise six months earlier Swami got lost, and it took them ten days to locate him and ship him back home.

Organized sports were part of the training program, but the students played games like basketball and hockey with an interesting new twist. The strongest psychic on each team would place a psychic shield over the basket or across the goal. The other players, moving the basketball or puck with their minds, would then try to break through the opposing team's shield and score. Peter took Edward to a hockey game in the senior league, where the players didn't even leave their respective benches.

"Watch the red forward sitting on the end. He's really hot," Peter said.

"How do you tell who's playing what?" Edward asked, as he watched the puck zip down the rink, stop and then make a sharp turn. Finally, he switched into second-sight and was now able to see the lines of force reaching out from each player and pushing the puck down the ice.

The blue team slowly edged ahead, intercepting a few key passes and breaking through their opponent's psychic shield to score. The red team was coming down the ice trying to tie the game when the buzzer rang. Taking the loss badly, they levitated the net and dropped it over the blue team's members. They were awarded the victory for this show of bad sportsmanship.

Although in class the students took their training seriously, they were still children and inclined to play with their newborn powers. Eating in the cafeteria that night, Edward looked up to see a fork of food floating up to him. It now turned over and the meatball fell to his lap. Edward looked around to see the others waiting for his response.

"Food fight," Edward yelled out, as the meatball rose from his lap and then whizzed across the room, splattering on the far wall. The others soon joined in, and before long everybody was covered with food. Edward had been the chief target of this messy hazing, but he was now accepted as one of them.

In the days that followed, while Edward came into close contact with the students, he questioned them about the aims of Peterson's program and probed their minds to gauge the depth of their commitment. Long-range plans had not yet been disclosed, but the children trusted teachers who had opened such marvelous new horizons to them. No doubt this was part of the master plan. Although the premature development of higher mind faculties bestowed great psychic powers on them, it also undermined their conscious mind's autonomy and its ability to evaluate and integrate heightened psychic content. This would eventually leave these children open to subversion from within by trusted allies who could penetrate their shield.

By the end of the tour, Edward had gained Peter's trust and they were able to talk freely. Peter expressed great enthusiasm for Dr. Peterson's program, but had misgivings about some of the mind control techniques they were being taught.

Edward now planned to fight them, and sensing an ally in Peter, talked with his newfound friend as they walked across campus several days later.

"Well, Peter. I'll have to admit I'm pretty impressed with this program, if unsure of its aims," Edward said.

"It's a perfect blend of Western technology and Eastern knowledge."

"I'd have to agree, but I wonder if they're not pushing your development too fast?"

"We're trying for a major breakthrough," Peter said.

"I gather, but my concern is for you and the others. Your powers are not exactly evolving at a natural pace."

"Dr. Peterson says we don't have much time left, and if we don't intercede soon, mankind will destroy itself."

"Well, it's said that the forced development of such powers by a small group of priests is what led to the destruction of Atlantis."

"They must've misused their powers, but Dr. Peterson

has very high ideals, only the world's best interest at heart," Peter said.

"I'm sure she does, but what gives her the right to decide our collective future, and use these awesome powers to impose her will on us?"

"She says she's been anointed by the 'HOLY ONE.'"

"Let those who accept that authority submit, and allow the rest of us to follow our own inner voice."

"She says she speaks for all of us."

"How can she speak for me without my consent?" Edward asked.

"She says that the rest of mankind has not yet awakened, and when they do, they will acknowledge her."

"But she can't wait, or we'll be destroyed?"

"How did you know?"

"Believe me, I've heard it before, and with more subtlety."

"You may find it easy to discount her claim, but I need proof of her error before turning against her," Peter said.

"All right. If she's been sent to save us from our destruction, then she must place a high premium on human life."

"Yes."

"And if she should destroy human life?"

"She would be in error," Peter replied, pleased with this criterion.

"It's only a matter of time with the 'Anointed Ones.'"

Edward was impressed with Peter's understanding of this crucial point, and knew that he would make a strong spiritual ally. Edward did not know how he would oppose this movement without the use of force, but that was one oath he would never break. For now he would join up with them, gain Abigail's confidence and work this way into a position where he could undermine this movement from within.

FIFTEEN

Dr. Peterson treated Edward's request to join their movement with skepticism. No doubt he was after something. To start, Edward was treated as any other candidate and given the same battery of tests. He went along with them and impressed everybody with his cooperation. Edward's P.Q. (psychic quotient) was the highest ever tested, and he could forgo training and be placed directly into field operations once they approved his security clearance. Although she was still suspicious, and Abigail wanted to believe Edward had at last accepted his destiny, she suspected his motives were less than honorable.

"This is a sudden turnabout," Abigail said, as the two of them talked in her office. "What made you change your mind?"

"Sheer boredom," Edward said, as he stretched his

arms and yawned.

"So, you're still unswayed by the nobility of our cause?"

"I'm all for world peace."

"But, as you know from past experience, the price will be high."

"You're levying taxes before you gain power?" Edward asked. "The Romans would've loved you."

"Don't get smart with me," Abigail said, as she stood up and began to pace the room. "Now, I don't expect the same degree of commitment from you, and I know you're unaffected by any religious appeal, but nevertheless your irreverent attitude could contaminate the other students. We can't afford that. So, I'm telling you now: you're either with us one hundred percent, or not at all."

"Great speech, Abigail. But save it for the others. I'll give you six hours a day, no weekends, and I want to be king of . . . Australia."

"Sold."

Edward was next given an extensive briefing on their upcoming war games exercise. For over a year, spies had infiltrated school systems across the country and planted seeds of unrest in the minds of America's schoolchildren. Next would follow widespread, massive resistance in the form of student protests. The present exercise was more of a commando operation aimed at a quick, decisive takeover of each system once the administration's morale had been broken. This objective required great speed for a precisely timed nationwide effort.

Edward joined an advance team of child psychics who now infiltrated a school system in the Midwest. The students had already staged a playground sit-in over excessive homework, a hunger strike over inedible lunches, and were threatening a walkout over Saturday attendance for snow-days. A team member was assigned each student leader targeted for mental manipulation. They now juiced up the young activists, fed them reports on the opposition's secret plans, and suggested a new round of sophisticated demands. It wasn't long before this accelerated conflict had completely disrupted the school system and brought all activities to a complete halt.

The teachers blamed the parents for not properly disciplining their children, and the parents blamed the teachers for filling these young heads with liberal ideas. The school system was on the verge of closing down, when the mayor realized that their school tax revenues, the least of which was actually spent on schools, were in jeopardy. He stepped in, and with only a few face-saving exceptions, gave in to the students' list of demands.

Abigail was impressed with this initial operation, but they did need to speed up their takeover time for the final assault. In the months that followed, operations were conducted in other parts of the country to refine their approach. Zipping back and forth from one commando team to the next, Edward was able to subvert these missions with passive interference. Follow-up teams, assessing the results, became suspicious of Edward's sudden appearance before each new setback. To clear himself, he led the next operation and broke the record for a takeover exercise. His method became the model, and Abigail immediately promoted him to general in the United Children's Forces.

With Peter as his attache, the two of them now attended the final planning session before the first all-out offensive. At Command Headquarters, Edward took his seat at the master control table with the other military leaders. They now watched an overhead TV monitor play the first tape. It was a protest in New York City where students, wearing gas masks, were picketing for indoor playgrounds. The next clip came from Chicago where students had crammed three hundred bodies into a small classroom to protest overcrowded conditions. In the last report, students standing around a bonfire in Houston were burning recently introduced textbooks with a conservative bias.

Next came status reports from field agents flashed on the screen at 10 pages a minute. Each report was more encouraging than the last. There was little doubt that the time had come to launch their crusade. Abigail looked around at her team leaders, who one by one turned down their thumbs.

"Then it's unanimous?" Abigail asked. The others all nodded their heads in agreement. "Are there any questions before my speech to the troops?"

"How much force can we use?" Herbert, who was nicknamed "The Hun," asked.

"First use mind-control, then catatonic suspension, and if that doesn't work, fry the suckers."

The children now pounded the table in bloodthirsty approval, and then stood up and drank a toast to their leader. Edward joined in halfheartedly while he looked over at Peter to gauge his reaction. He flashed Edward a thumbs-up sign to show his new willingness to work against them.

The send-off was held the next morning in the main auditorium. The first wave of commandos sat in the first three rows. The other psychics, who would follow later, filled the remaining seats. Dr. Peterson stepped out on the stage to a foot-stomping reception, and walked up to the podium. She took the microphone and began her speech.

"Today marks the end of your education and the beginning of the end for the adults who would stand in your way. You are the best and brightest minds America has to offer, the most extraordinary gifted children the world has ever seen. The road that lies before you will not be an easy one to travel; no generation has ever had to face such a challenge.

"But, seeing your shining faces, I know you will vindicate the great confidence we have placed in you. In only a few short years, since before your birth, the world has suddenly become a very dangerous place. The time is growing short, and if the children of America, led by you, their saviors, do not intercede, the adults will soon lead us all down the fateful road to self-destruction.

"Just keep our supreme goal in mind: peace and harmony among all children, and then...a new world order. It is for the children of America and of the world, their threatened future, that we now go forth into battle, armed with the righteousness of our cause, to bring the world at long last...PEACE. Go, and may Krishna give you a swift and decisive victory, my young Alexanders."

Abigail raised a clenched fist in the air. The commandos jumped to their feet, clicked their heels, and with raised fists, they zipped out of sight. As Edward was leaving the auditorium, Peter pulled him aside and the two of them now walked across the campus and talked.

"Well, you were right," Peter said. "Dr. Peterson's no better than any other upstart caesar."

"Yes, in the end, despite the religious trappings, it always comes down to a grab for power."

"But, if force and coercion won't bring about lasting change, then what will?"

"I now believe the only way to change the world at large is by changing ourselves," Edward said.

"I don't see how."

"What if the great forces that form us, that infuse us from birth to death, are interactive?"

"Our personal striving could alter the pattern," Peter said.

"Yes, and not only for those that follow, but for all of us now."

"That would be revolution by personal transformation."

"The only way to effect true lasting change," Edward said.

"And now, do we just step back and give Abigail a free hand?"

"I will follow a course of passive resistance, and in time I believe this stance will summon a moral force to our side more potent than any call to arms."

"I will join you, but if this should fail, I will resort to force if necessary," Peter said.

"We must all follow our own inner guidance. Do what you must."

Edward and Peter received their orders the next day,

and along with their troops, teleported to their assigned location. Unsure of their plans, but clinging to their new resolve, they faced a gigantic struggle ahead of them against a deadly adversary and even deadlier forces at work within themselves.

SIXTEEN

Within six weeks the first assault teams had gained control of targeted school systems in each section of the country. They now spread into the outlying provinces, and with media attention already focused on their movement, it became increasingly easier to air student grievances and compromise adult authority to the point of submission. Before long this initial phase of their operation was complete, and the stage was set for student protests to be directed at injustice in society at large.

From Washington Edward directed this political action aimed at the children of prominent leaders across the country. Team members at their private schools had slowly drawn each of them into the movement using whatever methods necessary. They were next placed in high profile positions and used as spokesmen for the cause. The news coverage had made them pint-sized celebrities overnight, and now the plan called for them to use their new status to attack their influential parents in the media in hopes of a public contrition and help with the movement.

In Virginia the daughter of a religious leader startled her family with her vocal support of women clergy, claiming a religious revival was impossible under the present patriarchal system. In New York the son of a business executive came out in support of higher corporate taxation to feed homeless street people. In Washington the son of the Army Chief of Staff called for unilateral nuclear disarmament before the military destroyed us all. In Los Angeles the daughter of a Hollywood producer picketed their Beverly Hills mansion in protest over his inane television series, claiming that moronic programming was undermining the nation's moral strength.

As planned, these public confrontations provoked private debates between righteous children and their conscience-stricken parents across the country. Many parents began to examine their own ideals and found them lacking. A few of the targeted parents, impressed with the early development of a social and political conscience by their children, helped the child leaders to organize the first National Children's Convention in Washington, D.C.

Sticking to his pledge, Edward was able to offer only token physical resistance to their convention plans but countered with day-long fasts and meditations. Peter found this stance increasingly difficult to follow and took a more active role. Breaking into hotel computer systems around town, he crossbooked the child delegates with other conventioneers for some hilarious matchups. When they began to arrive, the children found themselves sharing rooms with snake dancers, rodeo cowboys and video salesmen. Few of these delegates ever reached convention hall.

Thousands of children did arrive escorted by parents and teachers under psychic control. The average age of the delegates was ten years old, and they represented every stratum of the nation's social and political structure. The convention got underway with an impressive line-up of adult speakers, and by the third day the media coverage, though condescending in tone, was growing. Abigail planned more extensive coverage for the final night. Commandos now teleported into the master control rooms of the three networks' New York studios. They zapped the technicians behind the consoles and had them cut into their regularly scheduled programs to present the closing ceremonies from Convention Center in Washington.

The national viewing audience now saw a small boy, blondheaded and blue-eyed, wearing white yoga pajamas and carrying a rose, step up to the rostrum. He had been prepared for this moment with three years of intensive training, and with the pitch of his voice he could have easily shattered the microphone into a thousand pieces, but would now use his power to win over the minds and hearts of children everywhere.

"Children of America, and our comrades throughout the world. From time immemorial, each new generation of children has inherited a world increasingly torn by hatred and strife. As young idealists, looking out from behind crib bars, they have said: 'When my time comes, I will change all this, I will remake the world. I will make a difference. But, as we can see looking out at today's world, past generations have not lived up to the promise of their youth.

"Their idealism was stolen from them before they were out of knee pants, and by the time they left school, after years of adult conditioning, they had become people capable of making the same hideous mistakes. Will we follow in their footsteps? Allow our idealism to be stripped from us, to have our heads crammed with nonsense and our hearts pumped with age-old prejudices? If we do, I guarantee that we will be the last generation of children on Earth.

"To shape our own destiny, free from past mistakes, we must break the mold and start anew. We can forge a new future for all mankind, adults included, but only if we take control of our lives and assert our independence. We here today declare before all the world the inalienable right to self-determination for all children. It is a God-given right, and it bestows on us a sacred duty to a future we must save for generations to come."

This speech was met with a foot-stomping ovation from the convention delegates. A young girl, also wearing white yoga pajamas, now stepped up to the rostrum and outlined a detailed program of self-assertion for children everywhere. The audience applauded each point. The next speaker was Senator Hodges from California, who had agreed to address the assembly in hopes of building support for a presidential campaign in the distant future.

As the senator stood at the podium looking out over the convention hall, he had a sudden splitting headache that went as quickly as it came. He was now under mind control, and he went on to astound the television audience with a rousing endorsement of the children's program. The adults, who had been mildly amused by these cute children dressed as grown-ups and holding their own political convention, had expected the senator to put these little upstarts in their place. His endorsement added an unwelcome note of serious-ness to the children's demands, and alarmed parents across the country who recognized a threat to their authority. It also brought a number of bomb threats to the senator's office the following day from parental supremacy groups.

Edward watched in dismay as the convention came to a successful close. He had hoped that his noble efforts would slow down their progress, but the movement now appeared stronger than ever. That night, while the others celebrated their latest triumph at a local ice cream parlor, Edward climbed the Washington Monument and looked out at the city's lights in deep thought. He was soon joined by an unexpected visitor.

"I'll have to admit," Tolan said, "I'm not unimpressed with your moral stance against the movement."

"Yeah, it's doing a lot of good."

"Well, you do have to give these things time to perk."

"I just hope the response will be in time to have any effect," Edward complained.

"I take it by that you mean the desired 'effect?'"

"Yeah, I think I know what's needed."

"To know that you would have to know all that's involved here," Tolan said.

"Okay, I might come up short in that respect, but I know we can't wait much longer."

"Again, that presumes a lot on your part."

Edward shook his head in resignation. "So what am I supposed to do then, just sit back in total trust and allow these forces a free hand?"

"Edward, you are making progress."

Tolan took a deep courtly bow and disappeared into the night. Edward turned and once again looked out across this city of political intrigue and wondered where he would find the moral strength to resist his own great need to interfere.

SEVENTEEN

In the months that followed the children's convention, parents across the country began to organize a counter movement. They absolutely refused to recognize their children's right to self-determination. The whole idea was abhorrent to them. What would become of the world if children didn't absorb traditional values? It could turn into a place that discouraged early retirement. Parents faced with such a ghastly prospect fought back.

They formed Parents & Educators for a Tough Stand, or PETS, and soon mounted a nationwide campaign to publicize their own ultimatum. Among their infamous demands were corporal punishment for disobedience, mandatory summer school for delinquency, and on the home front half-rations for movement members. With growing national support, they next called for expelling student troublemakers, or at least putting them into the foreign exchange program.

When this last measure failed to produce results, PETS took a more militant stance. They now began to kidnap student leaders from school districts under the movement's control. The children were taken to motel rooms in the desert, mountain retreats, and shacks in the Florida Everglades. Here professional deprogrammers, recruited from the CIA, were given a free hand to extract information about the movement's adult leaders and their secret training base.

They first deprived their prisoners of candy and soft drinks, and when the children came down from their sugar highs, they broke several with tantalizing offers of sugar-coated treats. Holdouts were played big-band music from the forties, or shown television commercials from the fifties until their minds had turned to putty, and they would sign anything. The remaining hardliners heard biblical passages read by Charlie Brown calling for parental obedience, and were shown a film clip of Kermit the frog reading the Bill of Rights, excluding the first amendment, and branding the movement a communist plot.

The deprogrammers were fairly successful with child leaders under psychic control, and were able to gather information about Dr. Peterson and her institute in Houston. It wasn't long before governmental funding for her research began to dry up. This could be easily replaced when one could enter the computer banking system at will and extract needed funds. In retaliation a child psychic allowed himself to be captured and sent to one of their centers in Florida. Within three days he had reprogrammed the deprogrammers, and convinced them to call a news conference.

At the Holiday Inn in Miami, the three disheveled, unshaven men outlined PETS' unlawful kidnapping campaign to the press, and gave detailed accounts of their sometimes tortuous methods. Their leader, Joey Columbo, now read a prepared statement:

"I just want to say how sorry we are if we hurt any of these fine, upstanding youngsters. They are a credit to their parents and teachers, and I know they only want what's best for all of us. You know kids are people too, and we ought to treat them with some respect and listen to what they got to say. And again, we're sorry and we promise to help kids everywhere get what they want."

Further investigations of PETS led to the disclosure of other shady operations and fully discredited the organization. Within months they had closed down their national headquarters in Omaha, and the parents' movement suffered such a public setback that it soon fizzled out. Former members in controlled school districts were now required to recant their prior allegiance to PETS before being placed on the teacher roster for the upcoming year.

The children's movement appeared invincible, or at least unstoppable by any conventional means. Edward had watched, disheartened and saddened by their growing success, but he continued a course of passive resistance. By now Peter found this stance untenable, and was preparing a counter movement of renegade child psychics disenchanted with Dr. Peterson's new goals of world conquest.

Peter arranged a secret meeting with Edward at Death Valley to persuade his former tutor to lead the commandos into battle. It was a bright sunny day with temperatures well above a hundred as the two children walked across the parched landscape.

"Edward, I have three divisions of troops just waiting for you to give the word."

"The only words I can give are, 'Turn your minds within, win the battle there, and all else will fall in place.'"

"As you've been telling me, but they're just words, Edward, nothing more. What we need is positive action," Peter said.

"And yet what you plan is no more than a negative reaction."

"My motives aside, if we can crush the movement, I'll live with the karma."

"You'll just feed it energy and it will consume you and grow stronger," Edward said.

"If I should fail, at least I tried."

"...the easy way out. Go within, my friend, and try harder."

The two friends shook hands and zipped off to their separate destinations. What they failed to detect were the prying eyes, like spy satellites hovering overhead, of two child psychics clairvoyantly spying on Edward and clair-audiently listening to their conversation. When Peter's commando force went into action the next day, school systems across the country had been alerted in advance.

They met heavy resistance in the hallways, gyms and playgrounds of this evil empire. It was a bloodless war fought with minds and not bullets, but one that took a high toll with combatants falling asleep everywhere from mental exhaustion. In classrooms simple requests, like writing their names, was enough to put some students to sleep. Deciding what to eat at lunch made others drop off. In the gym, where the sleeping bodies were stacked, playing team sports pushed a few over the edge. School buses, returning with full loads of sleeping students, were sent back on the road equipped with blaring radios. At home few students made it through dinner before collapsing from the idle chatter.

The battle of minds raged on in what many would come to call the "Great American School Snooze." Finally, with most of the combatants sleeping, the teachers were about to regain control of the school system. At this critical point, Dr. Peterson decided it was time to bring in her star pupil. Brian, who was being groomed as the next Messiah, was a child with incredible psychic powers. At a secret base in the Himalayas, he had been undergoing experimental training to accelerate his development beyond anything imaginable. He was more than Edward's match, and would find Peter and his cohorts even less of a challenge.

Brian went into action at one school after another, waking up movement members while leaving Peter's commandos asleep. Place in catatonic suspension, they were shipped back to Houston and kept in cold storage until more sophisticated reprogramming techniques could be developed. With their students awake and the schools once again under the movement's control, the teachers wished they could sleep off the rest of the school year. It would get worse. With the children of American theirs, and with the movement rapidly spreading to other countries, the time was ripe for operation: MESSIAH.

EIGHTEEN

As planned, using the American movement as a model, children around the world were pressing for their own right to self-determination. At conventions held weekly in other countries, child leaders trained at the center presented to even more astounded adult viewers their own unique set of demands. In Egypt they wanted antiquity tours for the poor; in Japan they insisted on more foreign imports; in China they called for Junior Achiever Clubs; and in Italy they ordered the Church to give the Dalai Lama a popemobile. For now Abigail would allow each national movement to go its own separate way. At some later date, after Brian's ascendancy, he would unite all the world's children under one religious banner.

It was now time for Brian to begin his ministry. In his first American Crusade, at outdoor stadiums around the country, Brian bemoaned the lack of spiritual values in the upbringing of today's youth. Sports heroics took precedence over intellectual and artistic achievement. Career goals and monetary pursuits were foisted on children at an age when their future well-being would be better served in search of God and Self. The emerging political idealism of today's children was a step in the right direction, but a better world could never be built on such beliefs alone.

Children would have to go within themselves, Brian urged his audience, to seek lasting solutions to today's pressing problems. However, such a path could be dangerous without proper guidance. Brian had come to open the way within for children everywhere, and with his protection the one true path to self-knowledge and power was theirs for the asking. He gave them a special mantra to chant, and told them to visualize his image as he led the audience in meditation. Brian was now able to tap their energy source to enhance his own considerable powers. He then went on to perform one miracle after another, giving further credence to his claim as the new Messiah.

The rest of his tour was a great success. In community after community, he was hailed as a miracle child for his truly amazing cures. In time the call for more personal appearances by this popular young Messiah was even more than he could handle. At each upcoming crusade there were child psychics planted in the audience. When they came forward and were baptized by Brian, they would go out and perform miracles in his name. Next he opened his ministry to help guilt-ridden adults unburden themselves. At Madison Square Garden he held his first Grown-up Crusade.

Adults confessing their sins against children were healed of their afflictions. With reports of these cures, adults everywhere flocked to the Crusades in hopes of forgiveness, and were brought down to their knees in homage to this young miracle-worker.

Brian now began his first worldwide tour. In country after country, he brought solace and comfort to distressed parents and their children, offering them a way out of their conflicts. His was a simple formula: the only allegiance children owed was to the spark of divinity within them, and the only authority parents could claim was as guardians of that light. And Brian, as the Great Mediator, would arbitrate all differences between them. In industrial countries power-hungry adults clung to their despotism, but in underdeveloped countries Brian's many miracles swayed the masses who readily accepted him as the Messiah come to lead them through the generation gap to the land of peace and quiet.

After a year's tour, Brian returned to America and was met by a jubilant reception, a prophet come home, and now millions sang his praise. Abigail decided it was time for the next phase of Operation MESSIAH. They would bring together child leaders from around the world at the First International Children's Convention. Here, before a global television audience, Brian would astound his audience with a truly mind-boggling miracle to validate his claim as the new Messiah, then announce his divine mission: the establishment, within one generation, of a worldwide theocracy with Brian as the High Priest.

Edward was now convinced that they would succeed, if

only temporarily, in establishing a single world government under one religious banner. He knew from past experience that it was doomed to failure. How many attempts at enforced utopia had he witnessed? They all promised a world-wearied people peace in exchange for personal freedom, but closed systems cut people off from themselves. Any force that divided a person separated him from others and bred conflict. There could be no peace among people until there was peace within each individual.

In the past year Edward had resisted every temptation to intercede, and as he mastered each impulse he was undermining without knowing it the archetypal pattern that fed the movement's success. Edward now faced his sternest test with their grab for political power, as he struggled with base instincts that urged him to strike out in anger. Edward went into the desert and fasted for six weeks, contacting the deepest level of his being. Here he was able to transform reactive patterns that had plagued him in one incarnation after another. Those patterns were the same for all men, and by changing himself, Edward had in effect helped change the world.

His soul mates were among the first to feel the effect. In Boston Cara woke up in the middle of a chemistry experiment, nearly blowing up the lab. In Chicago Rana found himself wearing a dress, much to his eternal embarrassment. And in San Francisco Robate regained consciousness while lifting bus tickets for his homeless street children. Across the country and around the world, hundreds of Edward's soul mates, all locked into the same karmic pattern, were able to free themselves. They were now aware of the situation developing in Houston, and followed the crowds to the convention where Edward awaited their arrival.

NINETEEN

Child delegates from around the world were arriving for the First International Children's Convention. There were over 50,000 representing every national children's movement. The Astrodome would serve as the main convention center, and the three television networks were now setting up their cameras and lining up their communications satellites to broadcast the entire proceedings of the three-day convention to a worldwide audience. They had been tipped off in advance that this would be the most spectacular TV show in history, as rumors spread that Brian would ascend into heaven through the top of the open dome.

With the start of the convention, Edward and his soul mates took their seats in the first three rows surrounding the main stage. They now went into a deep meditation, and as each new speaker completely denounced the adult world and drove the convention delegates into a wild frenzy, they collectively resisted every urge to fight this mounting show of force. Children around the world, watching this spectacle and cheering each condemnation, fed a growing thought vibration that was driving many adults into early submission. After three days of mass hysteria, as each thunderous emotional outburst shook the very foundation of the Astrodome, Brian stepped to the podium to make his political power play.

"...we are the future of mankind...we hold within our hands the destiny of the human race. The time has come for us to build a new world order where the Earth's great abundance is shared with all children and not a mere few. Here we will give where there is great need and take where in the past there was great greed. But our main objective is to bestow upon every child his spiritual heritage as one of God's children. This entitles each child to his own share of dignity and respect. In the past we have petitioned governments and churches for the needed resources to carry out our great plan. But no government will open their parliament to us, or any church their doors. For they maintain their power with instruments of fear; with seeds of conflict they nurture a race of slaves to exploit and feed upon. They will not stand in our way, but will bow to our demands, because the power of God and the onrush of historical necessity is on our side. I have come to lead you to a new millennium of peace on Earth and brotherhood among all children."

Brian sat down on his ceremonial cushion as five huge video screens were lowered behind him. Here were shown live shots of many of the world's most historic structures: the Tower of London, the U.S. Capitol building, Lenin's Tomb, the Pyramid of Giza, and the Taj Mahal. Brian planned to give the governments of the world a demonstration of his supreme power in hopes they would cease all resistance and give into their demands. He now led his worldwide audience in meditation. Suddenly the buildings on the screen began to fade off into an etheric fog. The television commentators receiving on-the-spot reports assured their audience that they were not seeing special effects wizardry, but a divine miracle.

Edward and his soul mates had now begun to affect by their great restraint the archetypal source of Brian's great power. Suddenly, the buildings reappeared, only to vanish again when Brian redoubled his efforts. Edward's forces merely maintained their level. With his energy source drying up, Brian could barely keep his act together. Space-time, kept at bay until now, began to fold in on itself depositing the buildings in place.

The children saw this monumental foul-up as a sign that Brian was not the true Messiah after all. And they were so outraged by his deception that the child delegates threw a temper tantrum the likes of which no parent had ever witnessed. After they demolished the Astrodome, the mob descended on the international headquarters and dismantled it as well. When the delegates returned home, they disbanded each of their respective children's movements, and many dropped out of school systems still unresponsive to their needs.

During this period, Edward and his soul mates worked

with these disillusioned children to help them gain a better understanding of their true nature as infinite beings. They tried to instill in them the idea that there was a universal order, and when they had placed themselves in harmony with it, all their legitimate needs would be met. Most of these children, still much closer to the source than their adult counterparts, were able to see the wisdom of this approach. They insisted they be treated with equal respect under the law, but they no longer forced the issue.

Disgraced beyond recall, Brian entered a Jesuit monastery and began a life-long repentance for his sins of pride and presumption. Swami Watchagucha was deported, and upon arriving in India, he turned in his yoga pants and became a poor beggar to atone for the misuse of his sacred powers. Dr. Pudunsky returned to Russia, and for his part in the conspiracy, he was sent to a Siberian labor camp as prison doctor. Here he would put his biofeedback equipment to good use helping prisoners withstand the cold, vicious winters. Dr. Peterson was stripped of all professional affiliations and her sentence commuted to five years of community service as a kindergarten teacher on an Indian reservation. It was hoped that direct contact with these needy children would eventually bring a sincere contrition for her past exploitation of their cause.

Before Abigail left for the reservation, Edward paid her a visit at the suburban safe house where she was held under house arrest.

"And I guess you're here to gloat over your victory, you little traitor."

"To be a traitor, I would've had to fight you, but I didn't."

"You just let the universe do your bidding," Abigail said sarcastically.

"So you still feel that yours was the right approach?"

"It beats letting parents walk all over their children."

"You prefer that their children stomp them instead?" Edward asked.

"We were just trying to rectify a past injustice."

"By reversing their roles, and not working out a compromise where both of them could live in harmony with each other."

"And who would arbitrate such a compromise—you?" Abigail asked.

"Let each of them go within themselves to find that place where all differences merge into a single unified voice that speaks for all."

"Edward, you're such a dreamer. Your world will never come about. Down here, as opposed to up there, power rules the roost."

"People in touch with the source of all power need not impose their will on each other," Edward said.

"And you expect your voice to be heard by today's zonked-out kids?"

"These are tomorrow's children, already born with this message in their hearts."

Edward was offered a position on the United Nations Children's Council, but declined their gracious offer and disclaimed all public recognition of his part in crushing the conspiracy. Edward nominated Peter for the position, and he accepted it with the understanding that Peter could consult him on key issues. For now Edward wanted to spend time with his soul mates, who were holding the longest family reunion on record.

They needed to make some collective decisions on how to proceed with operation: Awakening. They had agreed to reenter the general child population and spread their message of hope at a grassroots level without calling further attention to themselves. It would take years for this quiet crusade to have any real effect, but if they had learned anything from Abigail's scheme, it was the merit of patience.

EPILOGUE

Edward was now feeling quite good. He had broken through to a new understanding that gave him an incredible sense of freedom and a peace of mind that had always eluded him. In the past, Edward realized, he had had a false sense of responsibility, and he could now clearly see that changing the world was for him an escape from the even harder task of changing himself. And when he couldn't influence people, he criticized their attachment to material comforts, their blind striving after fame, fortune, and power. This attitude only created more distance between him and the people he wanted to help but couldn't reach. He now realized that their misguided striving would lead them down the road of pain and sorrow to where the path to enlightenment began.

While Edward was at home unpacking from his

extensive travels, Tolan paid him an unexpected visit.

"Well, I didn't expect to see you again," Edward said with a note of pride.

"You no longer need my counsel, that's quite obvious, but something has come up and I need a little advice."

"Sure, I'd be glad to return the favor."

"In large part due to your outstanding progress, I've been offered a promotion," Tolan said.

"Congratulations, or is it sympathy time?"

"That's the question. The position is a Grade 2 Saviour for a planet in the Alpha Centauri system."

"And you don't feel you're ready?" Edward asked.

"It's a pretty big jump from spiritual counselor to saviour. I've always been more of a book person, and going through that whole process seems a little much for me."

"It could be just what you need, and besides, from what I hear, you're long overdue for a change."

"And what do you hear?" Tolan asked nervously.

"You could do with a little less theory and a little more application of your principles."

"Oh, God. So he has been making inquiries?"

"There's nothing to worry about, I'm sure, but I wouldn't rest on my laurels."

"I guess I'd better go ahead and take the offer."

"Look, I know what you can do," Edward said, as he paced his room. "Tell them you need another earth incarnation to prepare yourself, and since Mary's gotten pregnant, you can come in as my little brother and we can get you ready."

"Now, that's an interesting proposal."

"By the time you're twenty, things will really be moving down here, and you'll get a lot of practical experience for your next job."

"You're right, I can't think of a better place to prepare for a crucifixion," Tolan said and, with an allusion to Edward's condition, "Well, I better make my arrangements. I wouldn't want to rush things and end up making the wrong connection."

"Maybe you should try it, it's done wonders for me," Edward said half-seriously.

"I guess I'll see you in about nine months. Tell them to paint the nursery blue."

Tolan now zipped away in a hurry. Edward looked forward to having a little brother treading the same lonely path. He just hoped he could help Tolan prepare for the difficult task ahead of him. Since Edward would be home for a while, with occasional field trips for Operation Awakening, he would have time to spend with his old mentor. Maybe this was a test to see if he was ready to assume Tolan's vacated position as spiritual counselor. He hoped such a promotion would come with traveling papers to another sector of the galaxy. Edward just couldn't wait to leave the Earth behind for good.